STUM-BLE

BECCA SEYMOUR

RAINBOW TREE PUBLISHING

ALSO BY BECCA SEYMOUR

COMING HOME COLLECTION

Realigned

Amalgamated

TRUE-BLUE SERIES

Let Me Show You (#1) | I've Got You (#2) | Becoming Us
(#3) | Thinking It Over (#4) | Always For You (#5) |

It's Not You (#6) | Our First & Last (#7)

OUTBACK BOYS SERIES

Stumble (#1)

Bounce (#2)

STAND-ALONE CONTEMPORARY

Not Used To Cute

URBAN FANTASY ROMANCE

Thicker Than Water

For information, contact the author: authorbeccaseymour@gmail.com

Editing: Hot Tree Editing

Cover Designer: BookSmith Design

E-book: 978-1-922359-71-1

Paperback: 978-1-922359-78-0

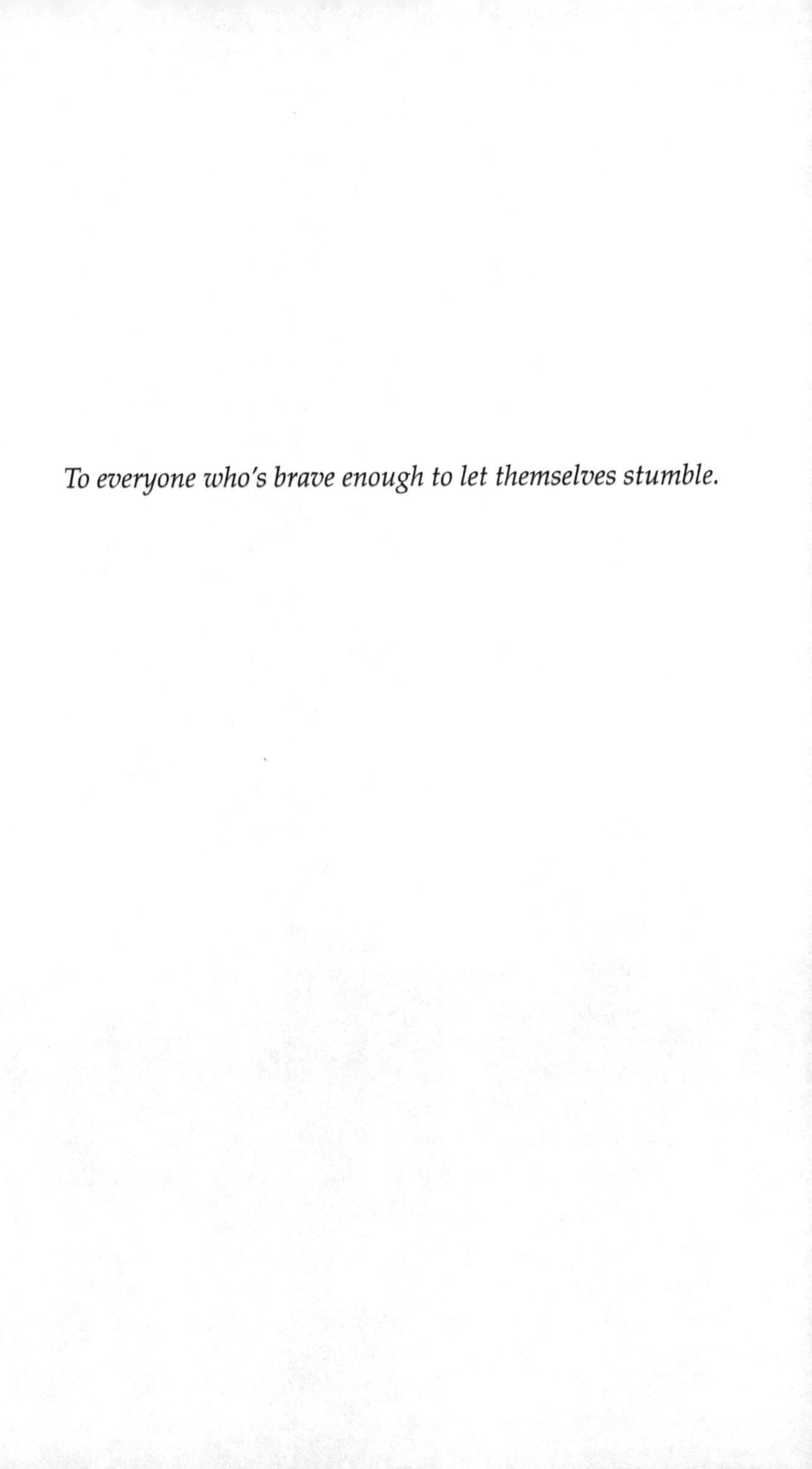

To everyone who's brave enough to let themselves stumble.

CHAPTER ONE

TREY

A lot had happened in the past eight months.

I could manage a five-kilometre hike without too much fuss. I could abseil a rock face with a genuine smile on my face, and I could even hold a conversation with Mark and not turn bright red in the process.

It was a decent achievement.

But this....

I shook my head and looked out the large glass windows, my gaze on the tarmac. This was verging on too much. My galloping heart was a good indicator that hyperventilation was imminent. There was also the likelihood of rocking in a corner spouting gibberish.

Gibberish was never a good thing, and doing so incognito would be near-on impossible considering my taller-than-average height.

"You doing okay over here, mate?"

The man who could turn my insides to mush and make me incomprehensible arrived by my side, his question making me jump. It wasn't one of those simple fast-beating-heart jumps either—those ones you could disguise.

Nope.

My whole body did this weird jerk, body-shudder thing. I clutched at my chest while my face heated like a furnace.

"Shit, I didn't mean to scare you." Mark's hand reached for me, his palm landing on my forearm. Meanwhile, wide-eyed, I stared at him, my pulse pounding loudly in my ears, my hand still pressed against my chest.

"Fark me, warn a guy," I said, finding my voice and trying to kick amusement into my words to conceal just how close I'd come to crapping my pants.

Mark grinned, his lips lifting high. I smiled back, unable to respond any other way, not when he directed his smile at me, playing havoc with my heart. "It's my day job of stealth ninja that's a killer habit to break," he said, chuckling.

"You need a bell, seriously… around your neck or something. You've got to stop doing that to me." I was only half joking. It wasn't rare for me to space out every now and then, caught up with whatever was rattling around in my brain, and for a built man, Mark really was light on his feet. Surprising really, since I was usually super aware of his presence.

"Sorry." His cheeks lifted, creating small creases to the sides of his eyes, just visible beneath his sexy specs.

And they *were* sexy. Mark knew how to wear glasses, and not in a simple "throw them on your face and be able to see and not walk into a wall" way of wearing glasses. He was my very own Clark Kent. Okay, not *my own*—a man could wish. But he was Clark Kent hot. I was thinking Christopher Reeves and Henry Cavill levels of sexy. Seriously, the best Supermen to have been cast.

I calmed enough to move my hand away from my chest, answering gruffly, "You're forgiven." I rolled my eyes, feeling like a dick but unsure of how else to respond. While it was true I tended not to turn into a puddle around the man beside me, it didn't mean he didn't affect me. Because he did, truly, and I was sure he didn't have a clue just how much.

"Thank Christ for that. Thought I'd have to ply you with booze to earn those words," he said.

I snorted. "The way I'm feeling at the moment, I am totally up for a beer."

He studied me a moment, remaining quiet, gaze roaming my face. "Come on. We don't have to board for another thirty minutes. Let me get you one."

I nodded and lifted my backpack off the floor, and we turned and headed towards the bar. "There's a part of me that should be arguing it's too early for a beer, right?" I said on the way as I dodged a few harried-looking passengers in the main terminal of Brisbane International Airport.

"But you're not?" Mark cast me a quick glance, and I side-eyed him, smiling and shaking my head.

"Screw that. My nerves are too damn shot to care about the time."

His light laughter followed, and a fresh layer of goosebumps sprang up on my arms at the sound. I was a sucker for a good laugh. I snorted inwardly, calling bullshit. The fact was, I was a sucker for all things Mark. Period.

It didn't take long before two schooners of beer sat before us, and I took a long and grateful swig.

"You weren't joshing me then?" Mark said as I swallowed and placed the glass back on the bar top.

"Joshing about what?" I asked, not sure what he thought I'd been joking about.

"About your fear of flying."

I gave a humourless snort. "Fear is putting it mildly. I told you I'd never been on a plane before. Why'd I bullshit about any of that?"

He shrugged, a small smile curving his lips. "I suppose. I just thought you were having a laugh or something about not being on a plane or whatever. Sorry."

"All good. Only me who'd choose the first time for a flight to be international and such a long-arse flight too." I shook my head, still wondering if I'd hit my head when I'd signed up to visit Utah in January for a skiing trip with our local Outback Boys group.

Skiing.

"Jesus," I said, not giving Mark time to respond. My brain went too fast, knowing in about fifteen minutes I'd be stepping onto an aeroplane. "I'm from the Sunshine Coast in Queensland, for crying out loud. The *Sunshine* Coast. The closest I've ever been to snow is staring at the TV and shuddering, wondering why anyone would want to be cold." I groaned and took another gulp of my beer. "Whose bloody idea was this anyway?" I looked up from my beer to Mark.

His smile was soft, amused. "Rhetorical question, right?" he asked, and I rolled my eyes and huffed. "You know, the first time I flew, I went to Melbourne and had a meltdown. Some passing air steward took pity on me."

I narrowed my eyes at him. "How old were you? Six or something?"

"I was old enough to know the guy was cute, enough for it to distract me," Mark said with a laugh.

I couldn't help but grin, imagining a younger Mark, all skinny and sweet, looking ridiculously adorkable in his specs.

"What seat number are you?"

"13A," I said immediately. I'd memorised the crap out of the location and its proximity to the exits.

A frown dipped his brows low. "I'm a few rows back. How about when we board, I see if we can do a seat swap?"

My heart flipped at his offer. "That's not allowed, right, because of whatever plan or something the crew needs?" I asked, really not wanting to get my hopes up that I could sit next to him for the long journey to LA before our connecting flight.

"How about I use those stealth ninja skills you're so impressed with?" He followed up with a wink. And rather than flip this time, my heart did a full-on double somersault.

It wasn't news to me that Mark was a good guy. We'd got to know each other reasonably well since I'd joined the Sunny Coast's Outback Boys and had spent countless nights hanging out and chatting when out camping or participating in whatever activity was going on.

But what we hadn't ever done was see each other outside of the organised activities, even though we didn't live that far from each other. Admittedly, us sitting in the airport bar was technically part of the group's outing, but still… there was something about him preventing me from freaking out and offering to spend twelve hours and forty minutes stuck next to me in a confined space that seemed different. Significant, almost.

And if that wasn't enough to get my nerves sparking for a whole new set of reasons, I had no idea what else would.

After all, this was Mark Hutchings.

Not only was he the star of every fantasy I'd had over the past eight months or so, but he was also everything I wasn't—excluding the fact he was perfectly gay. He was GQ-model handsome, fit, popular, and a level of professionally successful that I found intimidating as hell.

But as he looked at me with his piercing dark brown eyes and offered me that reassuring smile that I pretended was just for me, I figured now was as good a time as any to continue to push my comfortable boundaries and go all in.

Mark made me want to take a chance. That thought sparked my words: "You know, I'd love nothing more than you getting your nunchucks out and sitting next to me on the flight." I gulped, ensuring my eye contact stayed true. "I'd love it, in fact."

CHAPTER TWO

MARK

I was already aware of Trey's fear of flying. Just like I'd already known that even though I'd tried to stay away, I'd give in in the end and find my way to his side. Honestly, I was impressed I'd made it almost two hours before it was impossible to ignore his obvious distress.

And foolish or not, I wouldn't have changed my decision for anyone or anything. Not when his pale blue eyes captured my attention so completely. Teamed with his shy smile and words, which I could all but see him working himself up to say in a tone that portrayed confidence, Trey was the epitome of delicious and dangerous.

And I'd make sure I'd be sitting next to him in time for take-off.

"That's our flight," I said, referring to the announcement from the speaker system. There was no doubt Trey had heard the flight call himself. His stiffening body had been a dead giveaway, but I figured he'd happily ignore it and miss the flight rather than get up by his free will alone. "You've got this, you know."

Bright-eyed, he peered over at me, uncertainty in the depths of his gaze. It took everything in me not to reach out and offer him comfort, something I'd been debating from the moment—all those months ago—when he'd joined Outback Boys, unfit, flustered, and painfully shy.

When he remained stock-still beside me, I hesitated. Maybe it was finally the time to follow my gut and give in to the battle completely. Just maybe it would be what he needed to get him through the long flight. I ignored my rueful internal chuckle. Yeah, my desire to help him was utterly selfless.

Movement at last from Trey brought my attention back to him. His trembling hand was my undoing. I reacted immediately, reaching out and clasping his hand, stroking my thumb over his cool skin and not regretting for a moment the sound of his breath catching in his throat.

"Come on," I said, my voice quiet but firm. "Let's get this show on the road." I followed up with a smile as I stood, holding his hand tight enough to be clear I wasn't letting go without breaking off Trey's circulation.

"Okay."

I grinned when he spoke, not even surprised at the quiet confidence in his voice. Just because the man was a sexy combination of shy sweetness didn't mean his backbone wasn't made of steel. It was the latter that I'd spotted that first day when he'd completed the biannual intro hike—a short five kilometres, ideal for new guys intending to join the group.

Hand in hand, we headed over to the gate. I offered smiles at a few people we passed from the group, all openly doing a double-take at Trey's hand in mine. I was more than aware that me and Trey being handsy with each other would cause a stir. There were a few gossips in the group, and I expected they'd be lapping this up.

"All good here?" Frank said, one of our group's main organisers, as we stopped and stood in the queue to board. Frank waited at the edge, gaze roaming around the line, no doubt doing a headcount and figuring out who was missing. The guy was a teacher, so I imagined this whole trip and the organisational aspect were entirely his thing.

"Yeah, definitely. Just pleased the flight's on time," I answered with a smile.

Frank bobbed his head, gaze travelling to Trey. I followed the direction and looked to the man at my side. He was taller than me, wider set, his limbs strong, his stomach a little soft, and his grip on my hand felt strangely familiar.

Trey seemed to come out of himself, perhaps noticing Frank for the first time, perhaps that I'd stopped talking; either way, he looked my way, eyes on me, and then on Frank. "Oh, hey, Frank," he said. A tight smile formed on his mouth. "All set? Everyone here and eager to go?"

I squeezed his hand immediately, an automatic reaction at him bullshitting himself and those around him that all was okay. As soon as I realised what I'd done, I paused, waiting for his reaction. He didn't jolt, didn't freeze, nor did he squeeze back. Instead, his focus remained on Frank, his smile softening slightly and the barest of pink touching the high points on his cheeks. The subtle change was enough to get my heart hammering in my chest.

Shit, I'd waited for far too long to make my move—if that's what I was actually attempting here—if such a miniscule reaction could get me revved up.

"—to go," Trey said.

I blinked, tearing my gaze and my thoughts away from Trey, completely missing what was being discussed.

"Great. Just let me know if you need anything," Frank responded, a mischievous grin on his face and wholly directed my way. He turned and took a few steps back, already talking to someone behind us.

"You okay?" Trey asked.

I smiled immediately, shook my head, and gave a light laugh. "Didn't I say I'd look out for you so should be asking you that?"

He gave a half shrug. "Nothing saying I can't do the same for you, right?" His gaze remained connected with mine. And while it wasn't the first lingering glance I'd directed at the man, this was the first he'd held without looking away.

Before long, we were boarded, and I managed to talk Benny, one of the older guys in our group, into swapping seats with me without too much fuss and without the cabin crew noticing. Once seated, we buckled in, and I side-eyed Trey. It wasn't the time to be admiring his strong jawline or the way he gnawed on his bottom lip, since I expected genuine discomfort had him tugging it into his mouth. But damn if Trey wasn't hot.

From the first moment my eyes had landed on him, I'd noticed he was attractive. Since then, his attractiveness had sprouted wings and hit me solidly in the chest multiple times over. Each time I signed up for a daytime event or a night or a few days away, regardless of the location or the activity, I joined in the hope that Trey signed up.

And still, I hadn't asked him on a single date. Not even the notion of a friendly get-together or otherwise had been attempted. There was no excuse other than my busy schedule that I knew I could make time for Trey in if I really wanted to; that, and I was relationship averse. But with my ex still sniffing about even after a year, I'd talked myself out of looking for something serious.

My relationship status had been ticking that single box for a long time, especially as I tried to erase the last, albeit brief relationship I had. And taking the risk and messing up my pretty easygoing life had me shitting bricks.

Not the best of reasons, sure, but it was the only one I had.

"So," I said quickly, realizing I wasn't doing a great job of easing Trey's fears and keeping him distracted, "you come here often?"

The words pulled the laughter I'd hoped for from him. Trey glanced over, and I looked more fully at the man.

"Not really, no," he answered, playing along.

"No bloody wonder." I eyed the distance between his knees and the seat before him, wincing. "Not the most comfortable, right? Gotta love cattle class."

He snorted and shifted a little, sitting higher and creating maybe a two-mil-bigger gap. "Right, I can only imagine what business class or first class is like." He shook his head, brows raised. "These tickets were pricey enough, even at our group rate. Can you imagine the cost if you have one of those beds?"

My smile was uneasy as I nodded, knowing exactly how much those seats were as I'd flown in them often enough. Brushing aside my unease, I attempted to change the subject, even a little. "Even these seats will be worth it to get to curve up some snow, though, right?"

As I finished speaking, the captain announced to the cabin crew to prepare for take-off. I didn't think it was possible, but Trey paled more.

"Oh shit," he said, gripping the miniscule armrests. "Is that normal?"

The noise in the cabin was loud from the engine, growing as we sped down the runway, the plane vibrating with the velocity.

He slammed his eyes closed, scrunched them tightly, and I was sure my heart was going to bounce right out of my chest with how adorable he looked. I was sure to God there was something wrong with me for thinking that, considering the fear rolling off him.

Needing to offer him comfort and ignoring my inner voice laughing his arse off at my expense, I reached for him and gripped his hand, leaning in a little. He didn't even startle when I made contact. Surprise flittered through me, though, when he turned his hand so he could hold mine properly. I swallowed the thrill and my smile, saying, "You know, if you yodel in snow, it won't cause an avalanche."

His head flipped in my direction, his eyes now open, his brows scrunched and a confounded look on his face.

"It's true," I said, grinning. "You can yodel as much as you like without fear."

His laughter was abrupt, causing the hairs on my arms to stand to attention. "Maybe I need to talk to Graham about a yodelling competition one night. I'm sure I have the lung capacity for it. Could probably make a good go of it."

I snorted, trying not to think about his broad chest. "I don't know; you know Graham will have everything scheduled out to the millisecond," I said with a smile.

"True, but I think Graham's got a soft spot for you so if you asked…."

I frowned, taking in his words and thinking about Graham, one of the other leaders in Outies. "Graham's got a soft spot for everyone. He's a good guy and likes to look out for… well, everyone," I said, not sure what else to say.

"Oh." Trey's smile slipped, and he shook his head. "I didn't want to offen—"

"I'm not offended," I said quickly, softening my words with a half-smile, trying to ease the worry etched on his face. "I just didn't want you to think Graham was interested in me and me him. Heck, anyone." My words were out there, and I winced as a flush covered Trey's skin. His hand in mine twitched as though making to pull away.

This right here was why I was relationship averse. And none of it was deliberate. I said thoughtless shit all the damn time, which baffled me considering I ran a successful construction company, and in my role, I didn't have room for making blunders.

Before I could clarify that I meant anyone but him, the ping of the seat belt sign being turned off drew Trey's attention away from me.

"We're in the air," he said, his relief evident in his quiet words. He looked back at me, the frown from a moment ago replaced with wide eyes and a smile.

My shoulders relaxed. While I would be revisiting this conversation, it could wait. We had seven days away in the snow. Seven days for me to stop putting my foot in it and make sure Trey knew I was interested.

He was skittish enough that if I came right out and told him, I figured he may just run in the opposite direction. I had to play this smart.

CHAPTER THREE

TREY

I was wrung out, and my anxiety was through the roof, along with my exhaustion levels. But I'd made it. I'd survived the flight to LAX, regrouped in the airport for a four-hour layover before our connecting flight to Salt Lake City, and was once again gripping Mark's hand as we descended towards the runway.

But above everything, I was exhilarated.

Not only had I faced my fear of flying, a fear born from reaching thirty-seven without ever taking a flight before, but spending time with Mark, something he'd pushed for, felt really bloody good.

All of that, plus there was actual real-life snow beneath us. I couldn't look away from the glistening white blanket covering the mountains in the distance, nor the shimmering brightness as we grew closer to the ground.

And through it all—the sound of my pulse loud in my ears, my sweaty palm pressed against Mark's—I grinned.

"Can you believe how incredible it looks?" I said, dragging my gaze away from the window and facing Mark. His eyes were already aimed my way, a gentle smile on his lips. For a moment, my tongue stuck to the roof of my mouth, the intensity of the look directed my way hitting its mark. While not unnerving, it felt unfamiliar and a little disconcerting.

Truth was, I wasn't used to anyone looking at me the way Mark was, with such laser-focused intensity, and I wasn't quite sure what to make of it. Hell, my last boyfriend was a chump who'd ended up wanting me for free board and washing facilities. It had done a hell of a number on my ego.

"Everything okay?" I asked, not quite sure what else to say but wanting to break free and breathe again.

When Mark nodded and smiled, saying, "Yeah," and his focus moved past me to the nearing ground, I inhaled deeply. The past nineteen hours were at the point of making me delirious. I needed sleep and was beyond grateful we'd arrived late afternoon, American time. It would mean getting to the resort, freshening up, eating, and then sleep.

Just the thought had me yawning, wide and loud. I covered my mouth quickly and then shook my head, encouraging myself to stay alert.

I glanced at Mark, laughing lightly when he yawned too, and followed up by saying, "No yawning. Stop. That shit's contagious." He shook his own head, no doubt warding off the exhaustion.

"It really is," I said, covering my mouth again as another yawn escaped. "Urgh, sorry. I'm so ready for bed."

He nodded, looking as tired as I felt. "Me too. I forgot what a ridiculously big day travelling to the States was."

Before I had time to ask him about his visits to the US, surprisingly not having covered that in the hours we'd spent murmuring on the flight to LA, the sound in the cabin changed, grew louder as we were close to touching the runway. I forced slow, even breaths, closing my eyes briefly.

"You're going to be buying me a beer thanking me when you realise how right I was about putting those extra layers on at LAX, you know?" Mark said, his voice taking me by surprise with its closeness.

My eyes sprang open, and I glanced at him, studying the darker flecks of brown in his eyes this close. He was smiling, which caused my own lips to lift and follow suit. "Yeah?" I asked, and he nodded. "I just can't begin to fathom how cold it's going to be," I said honestly.

At home, I'd only ever experienced a few cold lows of minus two Celsius. But those were a few random winter nights over the year. And by midday, even when dropping so low at night, it was usual for the temperatures to jump quickly to the low twenties. And up until a month ago, I hadn't owned a winter coat, so this whole trip would prove to be one heck of an experience.

The bump jolted me as the wheels hit the ground. My hand automatically tightened its grip on Mark, and I clamped my mouth shut before remembering to breathe. As we slowed and taxied to the terminal, my smile returned. "I don't give a shit if you call me out for being a dag, but holy shit," I whispered, for Mark's ears only, "I am so bloody excited."

Mark laughed, the sound loud in the confined space, and pulling more than a few smiling gazes in our direction. When his laughter settled, he leaned into my space, saying, "Good. Being a dag seems about right, all things considered. I think we need to organise a snowball fight or something one of the days. There's a couple in the group I'd quite like to see with ball—" His eyes widened, and I chuckled as he continued, "Erm, snow, I meant snow in their faces."

I laughed harder, and he rolled his eyes at me.

"You're incorrigible."

My nod was immediate. "That I am, but you cannot go around talking about balls in guys' faces and not expect a reaction. You made it too easy."

His smile was wide. "Duly noted."

"And I'm a bit disappointed," I said playfully, earning a raised eyebrow from him. "With your ninja skills you still want to organise something and not go for a surprise attack?" I tutted and shook my head.

Shuffling started around us as we came to a stop, the seat belt lights deactivating. Mark stood first, reaching up to the overhead locker. I happily looked on, enjoying the view of his shirt lifting slightly, exposing just a sliver of tanned flesh on his stomach.

My bag dropping in his vacant seat startled me. I had no choice but to tear my gaze away from the tempting view. Mark smirked down at me, apparently pleased with himself from the brightness that had seeped into his eyes, momentarily making his exhaustion disappear. "Clearly I can handle stealth," he said. "You want to see me in full ninja mode?"

Did I? I nodded immediately, enjoying this playful, relaxed version of Mark. It was a hell of a lot less intimidating than the intense one.

"You've got it," he answered, backing away so I could stand. I stretched as I did so, my long legs and achy back grateful for the reprieve. When I finished stretching, I looked at Mark, having moved out of the row, facing him rather than the exit. He stood just a few centimetres away. Humour danced in his eyes when my gaze connected with his, and for the barest of moments, I considered just how great it would be if I could lean in and press my lips against his. It was something I'd thought about time and time again, but I wasn't that guy. There were too many nerves dancing in my gut, too many questions and uncertainties for me to consider. Mark would be so much more than a casual hook-up. Those I could dive into without overthinking when there was a need for it.

But this was Mark.

And his lips were just there.

My eyes caught his; not sure exactly where my attention had been before that with my dancing thoughts.

"Oomph." I was jostled from behind, my hand reaching out and snagging Mark's arm. As I lurched towards him, stumbling, he seemed to have the same idea. His free hand landed on my hip and gripped, holding me steady.

"Sorry" was mumbled behind me, but my attention was entirely on the man whose hand was on me and whose breath brushed over my skin.

"You o—"

I cut him off, pressing my lips against his, making the decision in a split second to screw it all to hell and go for it. It was the barest brush of my lips against his before I pulled away. His eyes were closed, and as I eased away more fully, they opened, his lips also parting a little before, thank Christ, his mouth curved into a smile.

Fumbling for words after my spur-of-the-moment decision, I landed on "Thank you."

Mark quirked a brow at me, amusement evident in his eyes. "You're welcome?" The question was clear.

A bubble of a snort-laugh spilled from my mouth in response. "For looking out for me," I said, figuring it was as close of an answer as I could give considering my awareness of the cabin—the movement and the noise—beginning to filter in.

"If I keep getting thanks like that," he said, "just give me a heads-up whenever you need my assistance. I can handle every stumble you throw my way." By the time he finished speaking, Mark was smiling widely. His gaze also moved to over my shoulder. "It's our turn. You have everything?"

I nodded, grasping my hand luggage and giving him one last look before turning and heading off the plane.

<hr>

HOLY SHIT, IT WAS COLD. THE OUTSIDE TEMPERATURE gave a whole new definition to my understanding of blue balls. I quickly stepped inside the hotel reception, stamping the snow off my feet. Admittedly, as soon as I'd stepped into the snow, I'd paused, lifted my head to the sky, and inhaled deeply before absorbing the wonder of the world around me.

Yeah, it was cold as fuck for sure, but even when shivering and wondering if I'd ever warm up again, I appreciated the beauty of the snow and the mountains surrounding us.

While I had no idea how I'd fare skiing, knowing we'd be heading out the next day shot adrenalin through me. I couldn't wait.

Nor could I wait to defrost from just the few minutes of standing outside, waiting for my bag to be unloaded from the bus. The warmth of the lobby greeted me. I absorbed the heat, welcomed it like an old friend. I didn't even mind so much that Mark, who'd sat by me on the hour or so drive to the hotel, was currently chuckling at my basking in the warmth; it was pretty much his reaction when I'd suggested us doing snow angels outside the airport too. Which we hadn't, disappointingly, but Mark promised he'd join me in making one tomorrow, and I was absolutely holding him to that.

I wanted to experience every single thing about this newest adventure.

There were so many firsts, and I lapped it all up, easily fighting away the exhaustion biting at my heels.

My attention drifted to Frank after shooting Mark a wry grin, not-so-secretly thrilled he stood close to my side and was taking the whole "me kissing him" thing in his stride. Frank stood at the reception desk, a bunch of paperwork spread out before him, and I smiled, knowing he was a guy who printed off every single itinerary and reservation, much like my parents still did.

"What do you think's going on over there?" Mark's voice appeared close to my ear, sending a delicious shiver through me rather than making me jump. No idea if it was exhaustion leading my reactions or vacation mode flicking on, I sighed into him, actually allowing my back to settle a little against his broad chest.

There was no doubt Mark could handle the contact, the slight shift in force. I'd witnessed many times over the past few months just how fit and strong he was. Just as I'd surreptitiously eyed him up every time he happened to be shirtless.

I held my breath when his hands gripped my hips, and once sure I could answer without sounding like a teenager discovering online porn, I exhaled and said, "No idea. But I'm sure Frank's all over it." I yawned and blinked a few times. The waiting around meant my body was relaxing, and my exhaustion was nudging me.

"Still the same plan for freshening up, food, and sleep?" Mark asked, his mouth close to my ear.

"Hell yes. I'm so tired I'm seriously considering getting you to shift that table from in front of that open fireplace and covering up with the rug." I eyed the roaring fire I could see in a room off to our right. It was temptation personified.

He chuckled quietly. "As long as there's room for me, I'll totally do it."

I smiled sleepily at that and stood straight, pulling away when Frank turned from the reception and made his way back towards our group of sixteen equally shattered Aussie blokes, all hanging for their keys.

"There's been an issue with three of the rooms," he said, managing to pull off a genuine, albeit tired smile. "There were six of you who'd booked single occupancy, and with the heating out in three of our booked rooms, that's no longer possible. It means we're going to need to organise a room shuffle to share double rooms for those willing. Cody at the reception said they have arranged single rooms in another hotel about twenty minutes away though, which isn't ideal, but doable." I inwardly groaned, since I was one of the people affected. I'd deliberately booked my own room, not caring about the extra expense, simply worried about not dealing with someone else's snores or weird peculiarities.

Truth was, I liked my sleep. Without it, I could be grumpy. But I didn't want to dick around and head to a different hotel. My shoulders sagged, knowing I'd simply suck it up and share. I had no idea who else was impacted, but Frank was in the middle of handing out keys to those already booked into room share.

"What a pain in the arse," Mark said from behind me, startling me for a moment and pulling me from my thoughts. I turned, putting a little more space between us so I could see him more fully.

"Shit happens, right? I suppose we should be grateful they've got enough double rooms so everyone has a bed."

"True."

I nodded, aware of different guys in our group collecting keys and moving off. I turned when there was a noticeable lull, the dip in volume obvious after so much talking and movement. My eyes widened when there were just Frank and four more of the group left. I swallowed hard. Mark was behind me, and I assumed he was booked into a single since Frank was sharing with Terry. Mark moved to my side, and I glanced over, willing my body to keep the heat from travelling up my skin.

Sharing with him had bad idea written all over it. Though my body didn't agree with that assessment one iota. Nope. I all but thrummed in anticipation.

His eyes connected with mine, and I dipped my gaze when he sent me a wry grin. "Single?" he asked. I nodded and huffed out a laugh. "Roomies?" he asked.

Still smiling despite my exhausted hysteria meshing with the anticipation of sharing with him, I didn't have it in me to respond more than another nod and a "Sure." Awareness still thrummed through me at the kiss we'd shared. But I seriously was too tired to be dealing with anything but the basics tonight.

"I'll go grab the key," he said, and I happily let him take control.

Not long after we're in the room, and the problem became immediately obvious.

There was one bed. No sofa that could be converted. Just one large bed that looked so comfortable in my exhausted state that I considered bypassing dinner, but the fact that there was only one large mattress had me swallowing hard.

"So…." I left my words hanging, not sure how to approach the shared-bed situation. All I was sure of was that I was knackered, hungry, and getting a twinge in my pants from just the thought of sharing a bed with the man at my side.

When I glanced over at Mark, he stood to the side of the bed, a mixture of amusement, exhaustion, and something else evident in his eyes. It was the latter that had me gulping.

"At least this way there'll be no chance of frostbite," he said, humour lacing his words.

I snorted, my shoulders relaxing. "True."

There was no doubt in my mind that sharing a doona with this man spelled trouble. The thing was, I just hoped it was in the best of ways.

CHAPTER FOUR

WHY HAD I THOUGHT THIS WAS A GREAT IDEA? BEING cosied up with Trey last night was nothing short of torture, especially when our shared room was a king bed rather than two separate ones. After we'd showered, eaten at a local restaurant, and then dragged our tired arses into bed, his heat had pressed against me, despite our bodies being carefully apart.

There was a lot left unspoken between the two of us, but after almost twenty-four hours of travelling, last night hadn't been the time. Nor was this morning, it seemed. Not with the induction being over and us splitting into separate groups since I'd foolishly admitted to having done this a time or two.

The truth was I'd been skiing and snowboarding since I was a kid. I'd taken regular holidays with my folks to the Snowy Mountains in New South Wales, as well as trips across to New Zealand in winter. And since uni and making my own coin, I'd been lucky enough to visit the US a handful of times as well as Japan.

Not that I admitted as much to Trey.

I was more than aware I was luckier than most, but that didn't mean I hadn't worked my arse off to get where I was today. My dad had made sure of that. From fifteen, my part-time job had been labouring for one of the crews in my dad's building company. Despite studying my OPs for uni, I'd also opted for additional study for my certificates in the building trade.

My father was a firm believer in working and understanding all arms of the building trade, and while I'd worked my arse off and at times hated the extra study when younger, I was grateful for it today. It made me better at my job and better at running the company.

But all of that meant I was missing out on spending time with Trey, who was on the green run while I ripped up the double diamond. That didn't stop my grin spreading though as the rush of adrenalin shot through my veins as I carved up the powder. The freedom of a fast run was heady. Exhilarated, I focussed on the route, trying to think a couple of seconds ahead, loving the pull in my muscles.

I turned, cutting into the snow as I reached the end of the run, a smile fixed on my face. Pulling my goggles off, I took a moment to simply pause and take everything in.

The sound of my pounding heart filled my ears, something I hadn't heard enough of recently. Life had been manic, work definitely taking over and stealing away my downtime over the past couple of years. It was one of the reasons I was so bloody grateful for stumbling on the Facebook group for Outback Boys based on the Sunny Coast.

I was not a guy into group activities at the best of times. While I enjoyed a good game of footie occasionally, getting actively involved in an organised activity was something I hadn't done since uni. And a group specifically for queer men, well, that I hadn't done before. At the time, I'd simply needed an outlet, and it had legit been a "right time" moment when I'd spotted the group one afternoon bored and surfing the net.

It was true I signed up to events arranged by Outback Boys more regularly since getting a hard-on for Trey, but a complete step away from work had been rare. So this trip was seriously needed, and I was going to make the most of it.

Starting with finding Trey and seeing if he wanted to have lunch with me.

It didn't take long to find him.

The loud holler drew my attention first. It took me but a moment to recognise the clothes, and the large man hurtling down the small slope was Trey, his scream indicating he'd forgotten how to stop.

As he sped towards the end of the race, the panic of his hand gestures was obvious. I winced, wondering if he would throw himself down or ram straight into the fencing. Down it was. He hit hard, and I squinted, admittedly snorting a little in amusement. That shit was funny. The day before we'd arrived, there'd been fresh snow, so there was little chance of him hurting himself, though lunging to the side the way he had was reminiscent of old Warner Bros cartoons or something.

By the time I hauled arse towards him, Trey was sitting up, wiping his face of snow, and saying something to the instructor who squatted beside him. Trey's laughter rang out, making me grin and relieving that little bit of worry I had from seeing him fall. Before I could reach him to help him up, the instructor, a man about my height and a few years younger, stood, grasped onto Trey, and pulled him up. Trey immediately slipped and stumbled, and only the instructor's grip, practically hugging him, kept Trey from falling.

I paused, brows dipping at the unfamiliar pang of jealousy erupting in my gut. The sensation was foreign and unnecessary. Not that Trey wasn't worth the reaction, but the instructor was simply helping him. I rolled my eyes at myself. My need to step in and be Trey's hero or some shit was ridiculous on so many levels. It was a simple fall, and everything I knew about Trey told me he was a man who would never need saving.

"Hey," I called out, coming to my senses.

Trey pulled away, finally righting himself. His pink cheeks darkened even more when he saw me. He scrunched his nose and then sighed loudly. "Let me guess. You saw me making a dick of myself, right?"

I laughed, giving a little shrug. "There's something attractive about a man who can scream so loud and know how to take a hit," I teased, more than aware of my obvious flirtation in front of the blond man to

Trey's side. Finally making my interest clear to both Trey and anyone else within hearing distance seemed my new game plan. It was no wonder I was still single.

My gaze was pulled to the instructor, who chuckled and patted Trey on the back. He smiled at me and then Trey.

"You're doing a great job. Just need to sort out how to stop safely, then you'll be joining your boyfriend on those double diamonds before you know it." He bent down and picked up his gloves from the ground. "I'll see you in this afternoon's session. You're booked in, right?"

Trey nodded, his cheeks still red, his eyes wide. "Yeah. At two, for an hour."

"Excellent. See you then." The instructor gave me a chin lift, then skied away.

Despite the fresh air and vastness of the blue sky above us, the atmosphere between us charged, felt thick and unfamiliar. Since yesterday's full-on day and Trey's high stress, plus the kiss and our spending the night together, it was no wonder there was this kind of awkwardness between us. While we'd known each other for eight months or so, the past twenty-four hours had changed everything. And considering the bewildered look on Trey's face as he looked over at me, it was up to me to step up and break through the tension.

I ran a multimillion-dollar business, for Christ's sake. I could totally be a grown-up when I needed to. "So, what does a guy need to do around here to make a guy scream like that?"

Or maybe not.

I burst out laughing as Trey flipped me off. I even bent double as I snorted at my own ridiculousness combined with the look of amused horror Trey shot me. I took a moment to unclip my skis. When I stood, I jerked back, grunting, my dying laughter starting back up again when a clump of snow fell off my face, leaving ice-cold drips working their way down my forehead.

"Hey," I said, laughing, taking in the vastly different expression on Trey's face. There was something unbelievably sexy about that particular amused, self-satisfied smile he sent my way. "I thought it was the two of us against the world when it came to snowball fights?"

Trey's smile morphed into a grin. "It is, but that one you deserved for being a dick."

I laughed as I nodded. It was rare these days people besides my family and oldest friends called me out on shit. And the fact that Trey had no issues with it was refreshing. "You got me there. Come on." I held my arm out, indicating for him to take my gloved hand. "Let's warm up, have a break, and I'll treat you to lunch."

He grasped my hand without fanfare, his smile intact and a flare of something in his eyes. If he was anything like me, I hoped it was pure attraction. Deciding it was my turn to rock his world, just like he'd done with me yesterday, as soon as his feet found purchase, his discarded skis beside him, I tugged him close. That his chest touched mine was an added bonus.

Not giving either of us time to think or hesitate, I leaned up the couple of inches necessary and pressed my lips to his. His lips were warm despite the frigid air, soft and supple. I eased back after the briefest brush of contact, not pushing it and definitely not wanting to take anything further in the middle of the resort and the bottom of the run.

When our eyes connected, relief had my shoulders relaxing. The smile Trey aimed at me shifted to something sweeter, his eyes holding tenderness I'd hoped would be directed my way since the first moment I'd figured there was something special about this man.

Rather than ignore the kiss to the extent of yesterday, I asked, "All okay?"

"Definitely," he responded a little gruffly, reading into my two words so much more, just like I'd hoped.

"That's good."

He bent and collected his skis, and I followed suit, though doing so without releasing his hand, liking the size of his palm in mine. And while our skin didn't touch, it was the act and the warmth of the connection that felt so damn right.

"Anywhere in particular you want to grab something to eat?" he asked, the two of us both nodding and smiling at Graham and Jerry from our group who passed us by.

"Just thought we'd eat at the café here, unless you want to change and head into the village."

"Here's good," Trey answered. "I can do without fighting to get out of all this Michelin-man garb only to have to get dressed for the next session. Once in a day is enough."

I snorted my agreement. "A pain in the arse, right? Bet you're starting to wonder why you didn't talk Frank into a beach trip. Only worrying about putting your swimmers on and slip, slop, slapping sounds good right about now," I joked while thinking it was probably a good idea we spent our time rugged up by swapping our January summer for colder climes. Spending a trip with a half-naked Trey for most of our excursion would have made each day in public crazy uncomfortable.

At least here, the freezing temperatures kept my balls and dick in check.

CHAPTER FIVE

TREY

THERE WAS A BRUISE THE SIZE OF A WOMBAT ON MY butt. I didn't need to look to confirm. The act of trying to sit without wincing was a dead giveaway.

"That bad?"

Mark's question drew my gaze to his. "That obvious?"

He smirked and gave a small shrug. "Just a little. The cagey sitting and the way you're thinning your lips sorta doesn't hold anything back."

I groaned, the sound a mixture of embarrassed and pained. "Tell me it's not gonna be like this every day, right?" We were only at the end of day one on the slopes. Not only was I still jet-lagged, which didn't help, but muscles I didn't know existed hurt something fierce, and I wasn't exaggerating about the bruise on my arse. I'd fallen arse over tit too many times to count.

I was buggered, and not at all in a way I liked.

"I have some muscle gel in my bag. Why don't you grab a hot shower, get yourself relaxed, and then you can slather yourself in it?" Mark searched through his bag as he spoke.

"Deep Heat?" I asked, not really wanting my entire body to be on fire.

Mark looked up, a tube in his hand. "Nah. I have some, but just Nurofen gel."

I sagged in relief. That I would have gladly. Mark could lube the hell out of me with pleasure. I afforded myself a small grin at the thought, heat hitting my cheeks as my mind went on a rampage.

Hell, even if we went there, my arse could not take it. And honestly, I didn't think I could handle giving it either. Just the thought of using my glutes had a fresh wave of discomfort rolling through me.

"You doin' all right over there?" My gaze met Mark's. His brows were dipped, and I saw honest-to-God concern in his eyes. It was weirdly sweet that he was looking out for me so much. Truth was, when I really thought about it, he had since day one of my joining Outback Boys.

Realizing I'd been quiet for too long, I nodded, offering him a smile. "Will be after a shower for sure. Just don't tell me I'm going to feel worse tomorrow, okay?"

He snorted at that as I headed to the bathroom. "Wouldn't dream of it."

I groaned. "How the hell am I going to cope tomorrow?" I glanced over my shoulder to Mark, who was stretched out, relaxing on the bed. Amusement danced in his eyes, a genuine smile lighting his face, and when my gaze remained directed on his mouth, I thought back to the kiss he'd sprung on me earlier.

As soon as he had, some of the tension between us had dissipated. My stumbling into him on the plane and pressing my lips to his had left me with growing anxiety. Yeah, he'd held my hand, been beyond kind, but doubt had seeped in. I'd wondered if he'd just been too damn polite to tell me he wasn't interested.

Earlier though, out on the slopes with the cold biting my cheeks, that doubt had been kissed away.

"Remember tomorrow we're going tobogganing. We're also on our snowball fight mission, and we have a trip out. It'll give you time to recover."

"That's a hell of a relief," I answered, the schedule emailed a few days earlier a blur. "You need to use the bathroom before I grab my shower?"

He shook his head, lazily raking his gaze over my body. A jolt of awareness zipped through me at that look. It was one I was familiar with, as I was sure I cast the same one his way this morning when he'd exited the bathroom wrapped just in a towel after his shower.

I nodded and headed into the bathroom, moving quickly, not wanting to sport a boner in front of Mark quite yet. There was no doubt I wanted that to change, and as soon as possible. It wasn't even that I was simply desperate to fuck around. I got out enough for hook-ups. But Mark was absolutely different. My attraction to him rode me hard and had done so for a long time. Now in the position where we could do something about it, I was eager to wash away the day and get my muscles working again so I could make that happen.

I demolished the burger and relaxed back in the chair. "That was good."

Mark bobbed his head in agreement. "Right? Americans know how to make a decent burger for sure." He took a swig of his beer and glanced over at Frank, who'd polished off his pasta, asking, "How'd you get on today?"

Frank's smile was immediate. "After catching my breath and picking myself up, brilliant."

"You haven't been skiing before?" I asked. I hadn't seen him in the same session as me on the bunny slope.

"I have, yeah, but it was probably fifteen years ago. Once I got back out there, went with it, it was all good," Frank responded. "How about you? I saw you out there this afternoon. You seemed to be handling it well."

I grinned. "This afternoon was excellent. I'm going to try a different run the next time we're out there." Despite my bruises and the aches, which had dulled to manageable post-shower and gel application, I'd loved the snow. The small slope I'd managed had been a rush.

Since getting into all of the group's activities over these past few months, I'd had plenty of adrenalin spikes, and countless times I'd returned home feeling proud of myself. But the exhilaration of speeding down the slope... I'd never experienced anything quite like it before. When I'd told Mark that earlier when we'd arrived at our hotel room, he'd understood immediately.

"Perhaps we can spend some time together doing that, if you want the company," Mark offered, drawing my attention to him and taking me by surprise.

When Mark said he wasn't a novice, he wasn't lying, but the man was massively underplaying just how incredible he was. After lunch, he'd swapped his skis for a snowboard, and I'd watched as he ripped up the white so incredibly, I'd been left a little awestruck.

"That would be amazing," I said, "as long as you won't be bored." There was little doubt the slope I planned to tackle the day after tomorrow wasn't anywhere near as thrilling as the mountain runs I was sure he was used to.

My stomach somersaulted when his hand landed on my knee under the table, and he squeezed. "I'd love to spend the time with you."

There was no point holding back my grin, so I didn't even try. "Okay, sounds good." He squeezed again, and I dropped my hand to rest on top of his, figuring it was time to go for it, make it clear I was beyond open to exploring this chemistry.

"Terry, do you remember those days?" Frank said, his voice exaggerated and gushy. I glanced over the table at him. He watched the two of us, a smirk on his face, chin resting on his hands. "Not sure whether I'm nauseous or turned on."

I snorted, ignoring my embarrassment and focussing on the whirlwind of Frank.

"A boner for sure," Terry said, not particularly quietly, throwing me a wink. "And on that note, maybe we should have an early night. I have a few… kinks that need working out." He reached out and took Frank's hand. "We'll leave you guys to it. We're meeting at nine in the morning, ready for the tobog- ganing. See you then." They both then stood, picking up their bill.

"You two have a good night. See you in the morning," Frank said before leading his partner away, and left me wondering how I'd managed to sidestep the full impact of Frank's scrutiny for so long.

"So...," Mark said, the word trailing off. I glanced at him, so very aware our hands remained connected. His focus was already on me. His gaze seared through me, snagging mine completely.

Why the hell had I waited so long to let this man know I was interested?

"You want to head back to the room, or would you prefer the bar or a walk...?" His tongue darted out, just a peek, wetting his bottom lip.

"I'm definitely ready to go to our room." I barely recognised my voice, so low and husky, filled with a need ready to explode if I didn't get my mouth on his.

Mark gave a barely perceptible nod as he stood, swiped the bill he'd previously organised to be split, and led me to the pay station. I stood quietly as he swiped his card, wishing the reader would hurry the hell up so we could get to our room ASAP.

Finally done, I led the way this time to the lobby and then the bank of lifts. It didn't take long before the elevator arrived, and we stepped in, a guy perhaps in his early twenties joining us.

Tension zipped between the two of us as we waited in silence, and I offered a tight smile to the grinning man who'd joined us in the lift.

"Get a good day in?" he asked, his American accent thick.

I bobbed my head as Mark answered, "Yeah. We're lucky we're reaping the fresh dump of snow."

I side-eyed him, wondering how he sounded so damn normal and unaffected. I was struggling to think straight. All my blood had rushed to my dick, making thinking difficult. Having a conversation with anyone, let alone a man we didn't know and who I was pretty damn sure was eye-fucking Mark, was near impossible.

"Right." The man tilted his head, eyeing Mark a little closely. "You ran the double diamond today, right?"

When Mark said, "Yes," the guy's eyes lit up.

"I thought that was you. You had some impressive moves out there. If you're heading out again in the next couple of days, look me up."

I raised my brow, amused. "Really?" The question fell out of my mouth.

The guy then looked at me, his smile dropping a fraction, his eyes widening. "Oh, shit, dude." His gaze travelled to our joined hands. "I didn't mean like that. Sorry. I'm here with my girlfriend, and she's green, is all." He shook his head, eyeing me warily. I understood it. I was a big guy. My size had its advantages at times. "No offense."

Mark's shoulders shook beside me, and I squeezed his hand a little tighter. "No worries." I had no idea what else to say without backtracking or making myself sound like a bigger dick.

"Sure," Mark said, his voice making my shoulders sag. "We're not out tomorrow, and I have a date on the slopes with this guy here." He nudged his shoulder against mine. "But maybe in the afternoon if you're around. I'll look out for you."

Relief seemed to settle on the man's face as he reached out. "Name's Brad." Mark shook first, telling him his name, and I reluctantly released his hand for a few beats, doing the same.

The ping of the lift followed. "That's us," I said, giving Brad an awkward smile as I all but pulled Mark out of the lift after me.

"Have a good night!" Brad called out just before the doors closed, at which point, Mark broke into laughter.

"Shut it," I grumbled without a scratch of venom.

He followed me until we reached the door. I pulled out the key, my breath catching when Mark moved directly behind me. His front flush with my back, his arms circled me, his palms landing on my stomach. A red flash of the card reader had me grumbling, really needing to get inside our room, stat.

"You need some help?"

"No, I've got this," I said, my voice breathy. I was spiralling fast, caught in the pull of Mark's hands, his voice, and every sexy thing about Mark Hutchings. Finally, the light flashed green, and the click of the lock opening set a new shot of awareness through me.

We stepped inside, still connected.

Fumbling to put the key card in the slot at the front door, I finally made purchase and turned into Mark, loving that we were close in size so I didn't have to arch down too much to get close to him.

My mouth latched on to his. Our lips slid against each other, opening and tasting and finally getting more than the barest of touches. Moving my hands to his waist, I gripped tightly, holding him close, and he groaned at the contact. Delicious heat swept through me at the sound as our mouths stayed connected, tongues sweeping against each other as he backed me further into the room. When my calves hit the bed, I tumbled, landing on the mattress on my arse, still connected, but that didn't stop the wince or pained groan from escaping.

"Shit, you okay?" Mark said, pulling his mouth from mine, concern shining in his gaze.

I chuckled. "Perhaps let's change places?"

He grinned down at me. "Your butt bruises, huh?" He waggled his brows up and down, causing me to shake my head at him.

"Just get your arse down here already," I said. My voice dropped lower, almost to a whisper when I admitted, "I'm not ready to stop kissing you yet."

Heat blazed in his eyes as he moved away to stand. In my next breath, he whipped off his jacket and then his T-shirt before tackling his runners. I followed suit. He then shifted to the bed, easing backwards and clasping my hand, encouraging me to come to him. I did so immediately, lust bolting through me when he opened his legs for me, rather than me straddling him. That was absolutely good for me.

Once between his legs, I eased down, not holding back my moan when our jean-clad groins met. I considered easing back and removing them, eager for more skin-on-skin contact, but Mark had other ideas.

"This is enough for now," he said, no doubt reading my dilemma when we paused. "You promised more kissing."

A grin slipped onto my lips, enjoying this softer, open side to Mark. While always kind and a good guy, until just yesterday—it still blew my mind that it had been less than forty-eight hours—he'd been reserved. Not quite standoffish, but I'd had no idea what was happening between us would have ever been a possibility.

"I'd hate to break a promise." I sealed my words with a press of my lips against his. The slow-growing heat almost immediately picked up as I sank into the kiss, loving every flick of his tongue, every taste I got of Mark. My hips jerked. He followed the action, pushing up, and I rocked against him. The friction and knowing how hard he was beneath the denim sent a shockwave through me.

A spine-tingling shudder racked through me, so I rocked even harder.

"Fuck," I said on a gasp against his lips. I leaned back immediately so I could get to his buckle. With shaking fingers, I managed to undo his belt, his button, and then his zip. My hand was already under the fabric and on his cock before he'd managed to release my zipper.

He fumbled as he unzipped me, my hand gliding over the heat of his erection distracting him. I grinned when I saw the wildness in his eyes. He lifted his hips as I jerked and groaned when he finally wrapped his hand around my dick.

But I needed to kiss him. Needed as much of his body connected to mine as possible. I leaned back, and with my free hand, I tugged my jeans and my trunks down to the bottom of my arse, giving him more freedom. "You too," I said, and he nodded, following suit. I then angled down, manoeuvring the two of us so we lay on our sides, our hands still working, still gliding.

Finally, I pressed my face closer to his, capturing his mouth. I breathed him in, and on my stroke down, I reached back and fondled his heavy sac. Mark whimpered in my mouth, the sound tightening my balls.

I drew my hand back to his cock, working fast, wanting to come so badly that I needed him there with me.

He grunted, hips jerking, lips pulling away as he moaned around a "Holy fuck, yes."

Our eyes connected for the briefest of moments before he slammed his lips shut and leaned back. Sparks shot up my spine before rebounding back until my arse flexed, my legs straightened, and release rushed through me and out into Mark's tight grip.

I inhaled deeply, gasping for breath, my hand relaxing on his spent dick.

"You doing okay?" I asked with a staggered breath.

He released a short burst of air before nodding, his gaze connecting with mine. A slow smile appeared on his mouth. "I'm alive, if that's what you mean."

I chuckled, the movement making his hand shift and press against my balls. I shuddered and groaned. "Holy shit. I'm sensitive as fuck."

He grinned at that. "Yeah, me too." He removed his hand, his whole body seeming to relax. I mirrored him before leaning in and pressing a brief kiss to his lips. When I eased back, he said, "Shower?"

"Is that an offer?" I asked, not quite sure of our boundaries and really wanting to know.

"Absolutely."

Affection flittered through me. Mark could just about ask anything from me and I'd agree. If I could capture his sweet smile and this exact moment where the spark between us was far from fizzled away, I'd do so in a heartbeat.

But first, a shower, and then I'd be asking him to apply that muscle gel this time rather than struggling to do it myself.

CHAPTER SIX

Last night was incredible. It had been a long time since a joint handjob had blown my mind so completely, if ever. And it had everything to do with Trey. The more time I spent with him, the more certain I was that not only did I really like the man, more than I imagined, but once we got back to Queensland, I wanted to keep seeing him. As often as possible if I had my way.

The two of us were far too big to be sharing a toboggan, but apparently, I was being needy and thought it was an excellent idea to squeeze behind him. The result was us peering over the edge of the steep slope and quickly realizing the logistics could mean we'd end up talking about the ride for some time. If we were lucky.

"You sure you don't want to change your mind?" A hint of panic edged Trey's words, but there was excited energy thrumming off him too. We'd been down several times already separately. Both of us had flown over the snow, racing down. He knew as well as I did our combined weight would have a different outcome.

"We don't have to," I offered, hoping he wanted to go ahead. An adrenalin high right about now and sharing the moment with Trey was something I could get on board with.

He moved his neck from side to side, so I loosened my grip on him a little, allowing him more room. I barely had time to react and grip before he said, "Screw it," jolted forward, and signalled for Frank to give us a push.

The shove had me grunting, the speed had me gripping on for dear life, and Trey's loud "Holy fucking shit!" followed by a loud holler of amusement had me laughing loudly.

We didn't race; instead, we flew down the slope, going a heck of a lot faster than I'd been on a sledge before. I peered over Trey's shoulder, keeping an eye on our route, aware we were gaining ground quickly, zooming past everyone else. There was no way we'd be stopping where everyone else did, those who came to a gentle stop. No chance with the velocity we were going. The large snow mound was startlingly clear as we grew closer—our barricade. And heading into it face-first at this speed would be painful and probably leave Trey hurting a heap more than the aches he complained about this morning.

"Shit."

"What?" Trey called, his amusement no longer audible.

"Trust me?"

"Oh shit," he said, a moment before I held onto him even tighter and threw the two of us to the side and off the sledge.

We hit the ground hard, rolling a few times. Trey's grunt echoed in my ear, his flying elbow smacking me in the face. My own grunt flew out of me on contact.

Pain pulsed in my eye as we came to a stop, me on my back, Trey half sprawled on me.

"Shit, Mark, are you dead?"

I coughed while giving a pained laugh. "Not quite."

He shoved away, looking back, his eyes widening when he looked at my face. "Crap, your eye. Holy shit, did I do that? I felt my elbow…. Christ, I'm so sorry." He was at my side, his hands tentatively touching my face.

"It's fine."

Both of his brows almost hit his hairline. "It's already colouring. You can barely open it." Trey's concerned gaze roamed over me. "Did I land on you as well, hurt you?"

The worry pouring off him struck me. "Hey," I said quickly, forcing myself to sit. "Other than a shiner I imagine I'll be sporting in an hour or two, I'm good. Stop stressing."

He didn't seem convinced.

"Honestly."

Trey gave me a reluctant nod, his expression telling me he was unconvinced. But he stood and helped me up. "Maybe that should be it for the day," he said.

I shrugged, controlling my reaction to the pain from doing so. I'd slammed hard onto the snow, landing on my shoulder, and it had given me one hell of a jolt. "Yeah, maybe." Already I felt the onset of a headache forming.

Trey reached out and took my hand, his hold on me gentle.

"Honestly, I'll be good after a coffee and maybe an ice pack," I said, wanting to reassure him while grateful I hadn't worn my glasses. That would have posed a whole other set of injuries.

"Okay, but perhaps let's take you to the clinic to check your eye, just in case."

"I don't think I—"

"Please, I'll worry else."

I gave a small bob of my head, deliberately moving it slowly. "All right. Let's get this sledge back to where it needs to go and head back to the hotel."

He all but sagged in relief next to me. "Good. Let me grab that. Just wait here a sec."

I waited, one eye closed, head throbbing, shoulder killing, yet still, I didn't have it in me to be miserable or regret a moment of the time spent with Trey.

How screwy was that?

"I KNOW YOU WERE LOOKING FORWARDS TO THE snowball fight," I said. "I won't mind if you go." Guilt was a funny emotion, and between the two of us, we had it in spades. Trey, while relieved the nurse gave me the all-clear with the order to spend the rest of the day relaxing, felt like shit for hurting me. I, on the other hand, felt guilty as hell for holding him back. This was his first trip anywhere outside of Australia. It was also his first time seeing snow. It didn't sit well that he was missing out.

"All good," Trey said, a more genuine smile finally settling on his face. "You've felt the strength of my guns. Everyone will be grateful I didn't join in and annihilate them. That level of destruction I'd be dishing out?" He shook his head, pursing his lips. "There'd be no coming back from that for anyone. Plus, the last thing I want to do is strengthen my reputation of taking big guys down."

"I'm happy to go down for you any damn time you want," I shot out, laughing, and grateful the painkillers had kicked in, so the sound and movement didn't hurt so much.

"Really? You're going there?" He rolled his eyes at me.

"You started it, talking about big men going down. You saw for yourself yesterday just how big I am."

Trey groaned loudly, covering his face with his hands. "Are you high?" He shook his head and reached out for the packet of pills I'd been given.

I grinned. "Nope. But I'm feeling more human, and you said taking big guys down, so what else was I to think other than you…?" I trailed off with a waggle of my brows.

"You're incorrigible."

I nodded. "That I am."

Trey grinned at that. "Okay, moving on," he said. I stuck out my bottom lip, ridiculously so. I would have had no hardship with Trey sucking me off. I was sure it would have made me feel even better. "How about we check out the spa instead? They have a couple of hot tubs. Hot water sounds good. My muscles are practically sobbing for my attention."

I quirked my brow at him, so many innuendoes dancing around in my brain. Instead, I said, "A hot tub sounds good."

"Great." He stood and headed for his bag.

"But don't try to go down on me in there. I don't want you to drown."

My laughter was muffled by a pair of swim shorts smacking into my face. "Hey," I shouted, still laughing.

"Fuck, shit, sorry. Your eye. I forgot." Two lines formed between his brows when he looked at me. I knew I looked a mess. My right eye wasn't completely shut, which was something, and I could see reasonably well out of it. But it was fierce blue already and unattractively swollen.

I stood and made my way over to him, pausing before Trey. "Don't sweat it." I angled up and pressed my mouth to his, enjoying how natural and effortless it was to do such a thing. "Here's your swimmers. Get changed, and we'll head out." He nodded, his frown easing a fraction.

After I grabbed my own shorts, we headed over to the spa area where the hot tubs were located. Being late morning and with the conditions ideal outside, the place was blissfully quiet. We snagged a couple of towels and made our way to the large tub.

I hissed in relief when I stepped inside. The water quickly covered me, already soothing my aching limbs. Trey was beside me a moment later, his own groan slipping past his lips. My cock perked up in interest at the sound. Not that I was in any shape to be pursuing anything; plus, even though it was quiet, we weren't alone.

"This feels amazing," Trey said, his voice deep and sounding blissed out.

"Good call," I praised, casting him a glance and a smile before settling back and closing my eyes, relaxing in the bubbles.

We remained quiet for a while before Trey asked, "When we head home, are you back at work straightaway?"

I sighed at the thought. Back home meant back to work. And while I loved my job, my position, I worked long hours, even more so over the past few months, usually making up time because of the weekends I took off every six weeks or so with Outies.

"Pretty much. I think we land at what, seven-ish at night?" I took his "Uh-huh" as an affirmative. "I'll be back in work the next day. In the office by six."

"Is that usual, that time in the morning?"

"Yeah. Our tradies clock off at four, though, but I'm usually there later in the office. All depends on what's going on."

"So are you usually in the office, running things?"

"Most of the time, yeah," I answered. Since my dad's semi-retirement, I was well and truly off the tools and running day-to-day operations. I had a team of supervisors and other staff, sure, but Dad had taught me the only way to keep in control was to make sure I knew about every job, read every tender, and visited each project at least five times over its life. It perhaps didn't sound like much, but we were a big company. The largest in Queensland. As such, we had multiple projects running on the go, usually with budgets above forty million.

It was no wonder I'd avoided pursuing anything resembling a relationship. Who the hell would put up with someone never at home? The reality settled heavily in my gut. The last thing I wanted to do was deal with real life.

"That's shit, man," he responded. "But, I get it." His hand settled on mine, startling me. I smiled and moved to properly hold his hand. "I can't imagine the workload and responsibility of all you have to manage."

I shrugged. "You get used to it. It means I make the most of any time away I can get." I squeezed his hand.

"I did notice you've been to a lot of the excursions and events. I think there was only one weekend when we headed to Carnarvon Gorge, and you weren't there."

The side of my lips lifted into a half-smile that he'd noticed. "A friend of the family's wedding."

He was quiet a beat before he said, "You remember what weekend I'm talking about?" Curiosity coloured his words.

It would be easy to keep up with the nonchalance, but Trey deserved my honesty. I opened my eyes and angled my head to look at him. His face was already turned in my direction, question in his eyes.

"I tried everything to get out of going, but Mum threatened to disembowel me if I missed it."

Trey laughed. "Why didn't you want to go?"

I scratched the back of my head, a little uncomfortable with the reality of admitting the truth. Before I could chicken out, I admitted, "I knew you were going to be there and didn't want to miss out on spending the weekend with you."

Scrunching his brows together, Trey shook his head. "But...." He trailed off before starting again. "You wanted to see me?"

I shrugged, feeling anything but nonchalant. "Since that first hike you attended, I've been interested, looked forwards to spending time with you." Rare heat touched my cheeks, and I was relieved we were in a hot tub, hoping my cheeks were already red from the water's temperature.

"With me?" Wide-eyed, he stared at me in disbelief.

I snorted. "Why is that so shocking?"

He opened and closed his mouth a couple of times before saying, "Well, I never knew, would never have guessed. You never said anything."

I raised a single brow at him and the hint of accusation in his tone. "What's that saying about the pot and the kettle?"

He stilled at my words. "What are you saying?"

"I think it's safe to say our attraction was mutual, yeah?"

A battle seemed to dance in his eyes before his shoulders sagged. I simply held on to his hand tighter, happy he didn't pull away. "Was I that obvious?"

"Maybe." I smiled. In truth, he was pretty obvious. I'd quickly discovered that Trey had a quiet confidence about him, which could easily be misconstrued as shyness. But he wasn't at all. Instead, he listened and spoke when he had something to say. But with me, from day dot, he behaved differently; only a fraction of nerves would flutter into his voice, a slight shift in his hand gestures. But enough for me to know he at least found me attractive.

"So," I said, feeling awkward speaking so openly about this. Or at least trying to. "I know my reasons for not sorting my shit out and asking you out or even for your number. But is there a reason why you didn't?" While genuine curiosity burned deep in my question, I winced on the inside.

Trey cleared his throat and glanced away before, almost reluctantly, peering back at me. He huffed out a breath. "Does it matter?" His smile was tight, his cheeks definitely redder than a few moments ago. "It's just, I don't know, talking about this... I don't know, we can if you want to, but—"

Humour burst out of me, and I laughed. When he raised his brows at me, clearly nonplussed, I shook my head and calmed down my laughter. "You're right. Awkward, yeah?"

He chuckled and rubbed his hand over his head. "Just a bit. Don't get me wrong, I suppose I can open up, but yeah…."

I grinned widely at him. "I feel you, seriously. Just thought I had to attempt to be a grown-up and talk about our feelings or some shit, you know?"

His gaze roamed mine, and he pursed his lips a little. After a beat, he said, "How about I just tell you that I like you, and when we get back home, I want to keep in touch outside of the group?" After that, he swallowed hard. I wanted to kiss the hell out of him for at least laying that much out there.

So I did.

He tasted of mint and ice cream from lunch. And as I stroked my tongue against his, I leaned into the kiss, enjoying the connection, embracing the need unfurling in my gut. I'd had some bad kisses over the years, but from the very first brush of our lips, we'd simply fit and gelled.

I eased out of the kiss so I could see his eyes. "I definitely want to spend time with you back home." Somehow I'd figure out my life, try to find balance. I wasn't sure how yet, but after so long of waiting on the sidelines for Trey, with kisses like that, he was worth it.

CHAPTER SEVEN

Far too quickly, the week was speeding on by. While I enjoyed every aspect of being in Salt Lake, it was Mark's pull and our spending time with each other that I loved the most.

We'd spent the rest of the week skiing, mainly together. And while I knew I was holding Mark back, I believed the guy when he said he didn't mind. I even had a go at snowboarding, which was hilariously disastrous and ended up with me in a compromising position with a flag. Mark said I gave a whole new definition to stumbling down a mountain, complete with a weave, and bounce, and a mighty big "Fuck, that hurt like a mother." Impressive really.

We ate breakfast, lunch, and dinner together, and ended up snuggled in bed with our mouths and hands on each other and not drifting off to sleep until my body was like jelly and I could see stars. It had never been like this before with anyone. And if this was how things would be between us, I was all in to try to make things work.

But there was also the reality of life back home. Mark had already told me about the hours he worked, and I had no idea how I'd fit in with the life he lived.

As a web developer, I had the luxury of working at home, a small one-bed apartment I rented, if I chose, but I was currently renting a shared office space in Maroochydore. I focussed better in an office environment. It meant my hours were more manageable at least.

It was our last night overseas before our stupid o'clock start in the morning. Earlier, we'd had our final session on the slopes and had later been on the Mountain Coaster, which was a whole lot less hairy than when Mark and I had thought it was a great idea to share a toboggan.

Mark's eye was no longer badly swollen, just slightly puffy, which he somehow managed to carry off still look. It was almost wide open, and the bruising was changing to a brown and green. He still looked ridiculously sexy. I didn't imagine there was much that would stop him from looking as gorgeous as he did.

And tonight, with him wearing jeans that hugged his arse perfectly and a form-fitting tee that he hid under his thick woollen sweater, I was having a hard time keeping my hands off him.

And he didn't seem to mind a bit as we stood as close together as publicly acceptable, waiting for our turn at the pool table.

"Did you sort out those calls you needed to make earlier?" I asked, aware he'd been determined to not pick up his emails but could only dodge a few texts for so long as they stated they were urgent.

"Yeah," he answered. "Put out a couple of fires."

"At least you won't have to deal with them when we get back."

"True, but I'd rather not be thinking about work right now." He leaned in and pressed his lips to my neck. Goosebumps broke out on my skin, and my insides melted a little.

"I get it," I answered, "but we've already made plans to see each other this weekend. So there's that to look forward to."

He grinned at me before taking a swig of his beer. "You sure you want to come to my place in New Farm and not go to my apartment on Sunshine Beach?"

He spoke so nonchalantly, as though he wasn't talking about the most expensive suburbs in Brisbane or the Sunshine Coast. But I took it in my stride, not concerned as there was no arrogance evident. "I'm interested in seeing your place in the city. Plus I don't really head to Brissie that much." I turned a little towards him. "Sorry, I just thought you're in the city for work, right, for the head office?"

He nodded. "Yeah, but that's okay."

"I mean, I understand if you'd prefer to head to the Sunny Coast to take a proper weekend break, if that's what you usually do."

He squeezed my waist lightly. "It's all good. The city will be different with you there, and I rarely get out since I'm only there during the week. It'll be nice to head out."

"That's good. I thought I'd just take the train."

Frank called Mark's name, indicating it was his game. "The train works for sure," Mark said, before dotting a kiss on my mouth and making his way over to Frank. He picked up the cue and broke, potting a stripe immediately. A shit-eating grin appeared on his face, and he glanced over at me, shooting me a pleased wink. I grinned back and then said hi to Frank when he appeared by my side.

"All good over here?"

I bobbed my head. "Can't complain," I said, sending him a smile before returning part of my attention to Mark, who was playing this game against Terry.

"So, would you do it again?"

Confused, I looked over at him. When he saw my expression, he clarified, "Skiing. You enjoyed it, haven't been put off?"

"Ah," I responded, smiling. "Yeah, it's been great. Not sure I've got the bug so will want to do it every year, but I'm keen to try out the slopes in New South Wales or Victoria for sure. Maybe next year. Mark was telling me about one of the resorts he's visited regularly. It sounds great. I definitely like the idea of a short flight compared to the one to the States."

Frank gave a small nod, his head tilting a little to the left as though studying me.

"All okay?" I asked.

His brows raised high. "Oh yeah, absolutely. So, you and Mark, you're looking at long-term then?"

If it was perhaps anyone else, I'd have changed the subject entirely or maybe told them to piss off and mind their business, but I didn't think Frank would allow the first, and I liked and respected the man too much for the latter. I aimed for a casual shrug, but I huffed out a breath at the same time, giving him a greater insight that there was definitely something on my mind.

"Want to talk about it?"

I gave a half-hearted laugh. "Honestly, there's nothing wrong. I'm not even sure what that reaction was about. But it's Mark, you know? Mark Hutchings."

"Ah, gotcha." Understanding lit his eyes. "And is it his name, his money, or something else that's concerning you?"

I felt like such a dick for overthinking this, let alone discussing it with anyone. But I trusted Frank and knew he'd be discreet. "I'm not sure, that's the thing. I don't even think it's the fact that he has money. He's not an arsehole about it, you know, and has never been since I've known him."

Franked nodded. "Definitely. I've known Mark for a couple of years, and if I hadn't filed his paperwork, I would have been none the wiser about who he is. He was the one who decided to make it common knowledge, actually, about which Hutchings he was. Just wanted to get it out there, so there were no whispers or second-guessing. And it worked. We've always had a good bunch of people in Outies. It's never been a big deal."

"Exactly, so I don't know why I'm anxious about heading back to Australia." When I saw Frank purse his lips, as if deliberating on whether to stay quiet or not, I pushed, saying, "If you've got something to say, I'm listening."

He briefly flicked his eyes, and I followed suit, not wanting anyone to hear our discussion, especially not Mark.

"Holiday romances have a bit of a reputation."

I sighed, my shoulders sagging. "Yeah, there's that."

"But not all connections that start on vacation fizzle out. Plus, you're on a good footing at least. You're in the same social group for a start. Also, you live in the same area."

"Well, on weekends at least."

"True, but Brisbane is hardly a big commute."

He was right, especially by train so you didn't have to contend with shitty traffic.

"But more than that, I've watched the two of you dancing around each other from your very first day when you joined us for that hike."

I rolled my eyes. Perhaps there was a time I'd deny it, but after Mark admitted he'd always found me attractive, there was no point. I wasn't even surprised that Frank had clocked on to it.

"I'm impressed," he said.

"About?"

"You not saying I'm talking out of my backside."

I laughed. "There's no point. We have been."

"And that," he said, pointing his finger at me for good measure, "is exactly why you've got nothing to worry about. Every hike, every kayak, every abseil and rock climb, you've gotten to know each other, even if you didn't fully realise just how well. You sort of always gravitated towards each other, even if not partnered up. A connection like that, nah, there's no chance of it fizzling out to a simple memory and a casual hook-up."

His words resonated with me. I knew he was right, but sometimes a little outside perspective went a long way. My concerns were things I'd address with Mark should I really need to, but from just a week of hooking up, I had no desire to label anything or put pressure on either of us.

"Thanks, Frank. I appreciate it."

He clapped me on the arm. "No worries. Happy to help."

From our group, Pete caught his attention, so he left, reminding me of the time to meet in the morning for the bus to take us to the airport. As if I could forget. While I wasn't as worked up as I had been for the outbound flight, I wasn't excited for it either. At least this time I'd have the warmup of the short internal flight to LA before the long-haul flight home.

I also hoped that checking in, I could upgrade to get some more leg room, as my long legs were not great pushed into the seat in front. I figured Mark would be on board, already having discussed our plan to ensure we sat next to each other again.

Turning my attention to the pool game, I grinned when Mark pocketed a ball. "Nice shot," I called out. His head whipped up in my direction, and he cast me that gorgeous smile of his that did crazy things to my insides.

It didn't take long to clear the table, Mark winning. He headed my way immediately, capturing my legs between his as I leaned against the wall.

"You proud of me?" he joked, quirking his brow.

"Yep, of course. Knowing how to play with balls means you get extra hot points."

He snorted out a short laugh. "Thank God for that. Not sure I'd cope with low score hot points, and you can always guarantee I know my way around balls." His voice dipped lower, and he brushed his groin against me. "You want to head to the room and I can show you?"

The conversation took a quick turn from me holding back my laughter to holding back my need to rub up against him and stick my hand down his jeans.

"Sounds like a plan." My response was low, breathy, revealing just how much I wanted to go to our room, ideally so he could get my balls in his mouth ASAP.

His lids lowered, dropping to half mast as he took my hand, picked up his coat, and started manoeuvring us around the tables. With my coat in hand, I used it to wave at a few of the guys, not giving a shit that we'd caught a few people's attention with how quickly Mark was striding forwards, clearly on a mission.

A few minutes later, we were in our room, already stripped, his cock free and his nakedness on display before me. I didn't even attempt to hold back my groan of desire. He was so incredibly sexy, all hard ridges, soft skin, and a smattering of dark hair on his chest.

I swooped in for a kiss. The touch could have easily been hard; it would have been if I'd listened to the ache deep inside me, but I wanted the night to be about him, about us finally taking it that step further. I parted his lips with mine in a gentle caress, holding back from forcing my tongue into his mouth and, instead, occasionally flicked out to allow our tongues to touch in the smoothest of caresses.

His gentle moans and pants filled the shadowed room, the small foyer our only source of light as he leaned against me, impossibly close. My hardness pushed against his own, and he arched further into me at the contact. When I angled my body from his by just an inch, he attempted to stop me. I laughed lightly against his lips, pulling my mouth from his and looking into his eyes. "Feeling impatient?"

He nodded, his eyes hooded, and his lips begging to be kissed. "I need you inside me."

I gulped.

"I want you, so fucking much."

Holy shit! It took all my restraint, something I was amazed I had, not to give in right away. I was on the edge of dragging him to the mattress and taking him hard and fast.

Not answering for fear of my voice cracking in desire, I returned my mouth to his. This time, I didn't hold back. Our kiss was fierce and passionate as our tongues tangled. I trailed one hand to his waiting cock and took the weight in my hand, loving the perfect thickness. As I kissed a trail down his neck, my second hand moved to his ass. I squeezed lightly as I latched my mouth over his pink nipple. Laving it with my tongue, I proceeded to suck. I was relentless in my sucking and nipping, spreading my caresses over as much of his skin as possible.

His hips pushed against me, seeking so much more. Removing my mouth, I edged down his body and cupped his arse with both hands. I looked up at him for a split second, revelling in the desire dancing across his face.

"I thought I was the one going to be showing my ball skills tonight," he whispered breathily, his amusement mixing with his obvious desire.

"Another time," I answered, my attention unfocused, wanting so badly to taste and prepare him. Without preamble, my mouth was on him, causing a loud groan to escape Mark. Immediately his hips jerked, unable to hold still.

He was long and oh so perfect. Tracing the underside of his cock with my tongue, I caressed his sack, earning me a delicious whimper and causing my own balls to tighten. I could do this all day, spend hours worshipping his thick length—the threat of lockjaw be damned—and I could totally get off on the sounds he made and the taste of his pre-cum on my tongue.

"Fuck, what you do to me." His words were soft and needy, and when Mark stroked my face, it was surprisingly tender. I glanced up at him, my mouth full of him. Intensity shone in his eyes. That look alone sent a new wave of heat licking across my skin.

I sucked in earnest and lost his eyes immediately as they all but rolled back in his head. Like this he was spectacular, and fuck I loved that I was able to make him lose his mind.

He got lost in the rhythm while I got lost in his taste and the feel of him. Eagerly I licked and sucked, bobbed and stroked. So desperately I wanted him to unravel. I wanted everything he'd give me.

When his breathing changed, his muscles becoming tauter, I reluctantly eased away, forcing my brain to think about more than my need. "You want to come now or when I'm inside you?" I asked, sure that was the direction this was going but wanting to make sure.

"Inside."

He gasped when I pulled away and stood, returning my mouth to his and backing him towards the bed. Then it was all heat... hard, hot bodies, tangled limbs, and connecting flesh as I caressed as much of the man as I physically could.

On his back, his lids at half-mast, his bottom lipped tugged between his teeth, he looked every bit a man letting go. My strokes were hard and sure. I ignored my shaking muscles and tried my hardest to calm the need to speed up and shoot my load. I wanted this to last forever. Wanted Mark to be begging me to make him come. Wanted him to gasp my name when he painted me with his release.

It was all too much. Too hot, too tight, too fucking perfect. Our ragged breaths filled the room and I groaned, loving every sensation racing through my body.

"You want my hand on you?"

Mark shook his head. "No, just, fuck, just right there."

I didn't have the ability to grin, the ability to pound my chest in pride that me nailing him so hard and so fucking good would make him lose his mind. My attention zeroed on making him spiral and let loose. The tingling in my balls were too sensitive; I was too close to finishing without him. And no way could I let that happen.

He deserved every stroke, every whispered word of just how sexy and incredible he was, and when he finally came, I found myself promising to always blow his mind. As the words stumbled out of me, I orgasmed. The rush ripped through me, sending those familiar stars dancing before my eyes.

And as we relaxed and I curled up against him, I couldn't help but wonder how we'd be able to make a go of this. I didn't have a solution, but there wasn't a chance I wouldn't try everything I could to make sure we worked out.

We fit too perfectly not to.

CHAPTER EIGHT

MARK

It had been three long weeks since I'd last seen Trey in the flesh, and something had to give.

The first weekend back, he'd spent the time with me in my apartment in New Farm. Our connection we'd found while in the US was as intense as ever. And we'd had the best of weekends. We'd seen each other several more times over the past few weeks, but since the last time—again when he'd visited me in Brisbane rather than me heading north—I'd been unable to make a break for the Sunny Coast. It was ridiculous. It was barely an hour and a half journey, but a health and safety issue at one of the apartment projects we were working on in the Goldie had meant emergency meetings and no time off.

We managed to speak almost every day, more of him doing the leg work than me. And it was that which I was sure was going to get old fast. Why on earth would Trey want to stick around with me, a guy who could barely take five minutes to shit without being interrupted?

This coming weekend, though, had been locked into my diary three months ago, and there wasn't a chance I would miss it. A day of climbing at Mount Coolum with the Outies was planned, and I was heading to my place where Trey would meet me.

I'd offered to go straight to his place, which I'd visited once, but since I lived closer to Coolum, he was keen to stay at mine, meaning we'd be able to have a bit of a lie-in in the morning. After a full-on week, getting up at seven rather than six forty-five was fine by me. While a lazy morning would have been good, the late summer heat meant we had to get out early to even attempt to get some climbing in.

When I pulled up to the underground car park, the gate opened, allowing me to drive in and head to my spot. I grinned immediately, seeing Trey's car was parked in my second parking space, having provided Trey with the access code before arriving.

After reversing in, I cut the engine and stepped out, Trey doing the same a few seconds before me. I hadn't even closed the door before he was in my space, backing me up and pressing his lips to mine. I welcomed the connection, as hungry for Trey as he seemed for me. That he didn't hold back, reverting to the sometimes-shy Trey, was a hell of a thing.

"Hey," I said, easing out of the kiss. "You been waiting long?" I'd suggested he should take a walk on the beach if he arrived much earlier than me. My apartment building was just a couple of streets back from the long stretch of white sand.

His smile was soft when he looked at me. "Not long at all. Like ten minutes. I knew you were close so didn't want to leave and miss you."

Once more, I swept my lips against his. "With a greeting like that, I'm glad," I murmured against his mouth. Reluctantly, I pulled back and glanced over at his car, saying, "You want to grab your bag and we'll head up?"

He nodded, squeezing my waist once before releasing and moving to his Honda. In no time at all, he was back at my side as I waited behind my car, ready to go inside.

"You not got a bag or anything?"

"Nah," I answered. "Everything here is set up for me. Even though I'm here less than I'd like, it feels more like home than the place in New Farm."

Trey nodded. "I did notice mainly suits in your closet," he said with a smile.

"Pretty much. That and my high-vis stuff for when I'm on site." I reached out and took his hand, relaxing even more when it settled there so naturally. "It feels too long since I saw you last," I admitted, too happy with seeing Trey and touching him to hold back my feelings.

He side nudged me a little as we waited for the lift to arrive. His scent, even partially hidden in the car fumes, wrapped around me, soothing my soul that little bit more.

"No argument from me," he said. "Never knew three weeks could feel like months before."

I side-eyed him, noting he looked away, but I still spotted the light pink on his neck and cheeks. There was no doubt I knew exactly what he meant, just like I understood his heated cheeks. Speaking about shit like this had always been out of my comfort zone.

Already I felt as though I'd opened up to Trey more than anyone.

"You want to head out for food, or we can grab a takeaway?" I asked once we stepped into the lift and I pressed my key card on the pad.

"Honestly, as long as food isn't in our immediate plans, I'm easy."

I looped an arm around his waist. "I need a shower. You're welcome to join me." I angled to lean in and press my lips against his mouth, inhaling his light aftershave and soap. I expected he'd showered before he'd left Maroochydore. My dick jerked at the thought, knowing he liked to prepare himself thoroughly for me.

When we stepped out of the lift, Trey looked around. His brows lifted high. "There's... this has taken us directly into your apartment?"

I nodded. "Yeah. This is the top floor. There's another lift on the other side of the building for the second apartment on this floor. The other two floors have three smaller apartments." Moving further into the room, I motioned him to enter more fully, wondering what he'd think of my place. Sure it was modern, but it felt like home.

"Oh, wow."

I waited for him to take it all in as he stepped closer to the open space's main living area. The balcony wrapped around two full walls of the living space. It actually continued along the one entire wall of the master bedroom too.

"Holy shit. This view is incredible."

"It's what completely sold me," I answered as we stepped out into the warm sea air, the views of the beach and the glistening ocean before us. I'd always loved the sea and the beach and was grateful I'd been brought up on the coast rather than in Brissie. The city was great, but between the open space, the startling blue water, and the freedom that it offered, this place had always called to me.

"Let's take your bag to the bedroom."

Trey nodded, his eyes firmly on the ocean. I understood the pull and the reluctance to look away when such a stunning image was before you. After a beat, he turned towards me, his gaze lifting. Wide-eyed, he asked, "Is that a roof terrace?"

I bobbed my head. "The staircase is just next to the lift. It's private. Set up for entertaining."

Wonder filled his gaze.

"I can show you in a while if you want."

He remained quiet as I led him to the bedroom, and I wasn't quite sure what was going on in his head. Once in my bedroom, I winced when I took in the space, knowing perhaps it was a bit out there, or maybe even flamboyant, but in my defence, I bought off-plan, and the large jacuzzi tub and twin sinks situated in the large bedroom were part of the plans. The toilet was in a small enclosed area to the right, close to the closet.

But despite it all, it didn't look like a show home, or at least I didn't think it did.

Artwork and framed photographs of my family, mainly, and a few friends lined the walls and the bookcase. One wall was painted a bright teal, the others oatmeal. A flat-screen TV was positioned on the wall opposite the bed, and a two-seater sofa, built for comfort rather than how it matched the room, was placed facing the floor-to-ceiling windows lining one side of the room, the balcony doors just to the side. The expanse of the ocean was the perfect back-drop for my favourite space.

While the rest of my apartment was bright white and minimal and looking very much a show home, this space I thought was more me. And it didn't scream coastal. It was clean and tidy though, courtesy of the cleaning service I used once a week.

I peered over at Trey, relieved to see him smiling.

"Thank Christ," he said, a small laugh huffing out of him.

"What?" Confusion flittered through me.

"This room has your stamp on it. It's you." He smiled as he looked at me, a softness in his eyes. "Everything else is just so… white and pristine." He followed up with a small chuckle. "And on the balcony, seeing your apartment, which is beyond incredible, it hit me just how loaded you are." He shook his head. "And I'm sorry if I sound like a dick for saying that, but I knew you were, had seen your place in New Farm, but that felt more like I was on a city break, you know?"

I nodded. I did know. There was no personality in the place, for sure.

"And then here, that view, this place… shit, it's so not my world."

I tried to stop my muscles from freezing as he spoke, his quiet amusement the only thing stopping me from worrying where he was going with this. Remaining silent was a struggle, but I stayed strong, listening intently.

"And then there's this room, your bedroom." His gaze roamed the room before returning to my face. "It's a good room." He nodded and huffed a laugh. I remained confused, but he seemed happy enough, so I wasn't sure if I wanted to question it.

When he didn't speak again, I hesitated before saying, "I like it. It's more me, you know?"

Trey bobbed his head. "I can tell."

I sighed, frustrated that the heat from our greeting had dissipated with the tour and Trey's uncertainty. The last thing I wanted to do was get heavy. I liked the guy, for sure. Did we have a chance of a future together? For the first time ever, I felt sure there was a possibility.

"Listen—"

"Shit, that already sounds serious. I was weird, right? I'm s—"

"No, it's fine." I cut him off. "Come and sit. Fair warning, you may not want to get up, though. It's the best sofa ever," I said, trying to lighten the mood.

His shoulders relaxed a little as he said, "So you don't think I'll be persuaded to hop in the shower with you?" He looked around, frowning. "I don't actually see a shower, but that tub looks pretty damn inviting."

I laughed, taking a seat and exhaling as I sank into the cushions. I angled slightly, so when Trey joined me, I could see him. "Oh, I'm sure I can persuade you. And there's a shower in the main bathroom."

"It's one of those huge monster showers, isn't it?" Trey smirked as he spoke.

"Well, it's only fitting since I have a mons—"

His snort cut me off. We settled into the quiet of the room, and I wished I'd opened the doors to the balcony before we'd sat so I could hear the sea, but I was being ridiculous, looking for distractions.

It wasn't lost on me that from having to be in charge and on the ball all damn day at work, in my personal life, I was more hesitant to push and make things happen at times. It was so much easier to let go of the reins and roll with it. But easy didn't always mean good or happy.

Forcing myself out of my comfort zone, I broached the subject that clearly Trey had on his mind. "Does where I live, what I own, hell, what I do bother you?" I asked. The last thing I wanted was to sound like a prick, but getting this out there now was the only way forwards. With my gaze on his, I searched for any cues, any tells for how he was feeling. Since I was used to dealing with tradies, who tended to disguise any hint of emotion with a cuss or a hand gesture, I didn't have a great deal of experience at reading people when it came to shit like this.

"I just," I continued, shifting a little more and stretching my arm on the back cushion, not quite close enough to touch, but near enough for now, "there've been a few times you've seemed, I don't know, uncomfortable or something."

Wide-eyed, his face flushed, and he shook his head. "No, it's not that, and it sounds like I made you feel uncomfortable if you're saying this to me." I made to speak, but he stopped me with his arm joining mine, his hand resting on my arm. "We've known each other, what, ten months or so?" I nodded, deciding not to tell him a quick look at my calendar, and I could give him the exact date. "I think it's safe to say

I know you. Not brilliantly yet, or inside and out or anything, but well enough, especially since America.

"I know you work your arse off, too hard, truth be told. And I know your dad built the business up, and I also know you've earned your position."

A rush of pride swept over me at his words, taking me by surprise. Hell, he was near enough saying he was proud of me. The warmth was heady, foreign that someone who wasn't my parents would see me for more than the boss, the bigwig's son, the guy in the suit and the hard hat.

"And alongside all of that, you're somehow not arrogant." I raised my brows at his words, and he laughed, saying, "Okay, not completely arrogant unless you're talking about the size of your dick." He rolled his eyes, and I angled my arm a little to touch him properly.

"What I'm saying is that it's all just a bit different, but I'm taking it in my stride. You're not a guy who flaunts what he has. And don't even mention what's in your pants," he said quickly, much to my amusement. "But I'm used to living very simply, frugally even, so yeah, just give me time to let it sink in so I don't even see it anymore. So, no, nothing about"— he gestured behind him and at the incredible view before us—"this is anything I'm concerned about. And honestly, I just don't ever want to come across as not paying my way. Being a moocher is not something I ever want to be." He huffed out a breath, those last words surprising me.

"I'd never think that of you," I said vehemently.

His smile softened, and he squeezed my arm lightly. "I know you wouldn't."

"But if I'm taking us out, somewhere I've recommended, then it's up to me to cover the bill," I clarified.

"Okay." He drew the word out. "And I can get my head around that and not tally up and overthink."

Concern resettled in my chest now that we were getting to the truth of what had been bothering him. "What's between us, how we live, how we decide to spend our time together should never be tit for tat. I don't want us running a score sheet, or an expenditure sheet or something."

Trey winced. "I'm sorry. It sounds screwy, I know, but I'll be honest, a couple of years back, I dated a guy for a few months. I live comfortably, you know, but not a life of luxury. Anyway, he basically took me for a ride. I didn't mind footing the bill, even when I always seemed to be doing it. He had a job but earned less than me, so it wasn't a big deal. But then he started to ask for things, asking to cover him for a new tee or shoes or whatever when we were out. Sometimes saying he was short on rent, and that eventually turned into him moving in with me for a while." He shook his head while unease swirled around me. I hated that Trey had been hurt. "Long story short, he was taking advantage, pretty much ripping me off. And was doing the same to at least two other 'boyfriends' that I know of."

"What a wanker." I scowled, wondering what kind of low life could target Trey, who was one of the best men I'd ever known.

"I just never want to be in a position when I'm accused of being Cedar."

"Huh?"

A snort escaped from Trey, his amusement much nicer to see and going a long way to unravelling my tension. "That was his name. I just don't ever want to be *that* guy."

I nodded. "You could never be that guy. Your wood's pretty impressive, don't get me wrong."

"Seriously?"

I laughed. "What? It's been three weeks." And sitting so close to him, especially with the whirlwind of emotions from this heavy talk, made it difficult to concentrate. Was it wrong I just wanted to stop and make good on the promise of a shower?

But before we could move on and hopefully put this shit to rest for good, I said, "I mean it when I said you could never be that guy. But money doesn't have anything to do with our relationship. It doesn't impact on our equality, doesn't negate our respect for each other. I'm not being a dick saying money isn't important... it makes the world go around and all that, but it's not even on our agenda for you and me, and it never needs to be. Sound about right?"

"Yeah, sounds right." This time he was beaming at me, and I promised myself right then to make sure we never went so long without seeing each other again. That was how stuff brewed to overboiling when we didn't get the chance to simply be with each other.

"I think we totally deserve a beer after this sharing shit."

"I think you're right," I said. Rather than standing straight away, I leaned closer to Trey and manoeuvred to straddle his thighs.

When his wide eyes filled with heat, I knew two things. One, this was the right move to get close to him so we could kiss the real talk out of the way, and two, it was quite possible my heart was getting comfortable. But rather than the knowledge having me shitting bricks, excitement stirred in my gut.

Possibility was a heady thing.

CHAPTER NINE

TREY

"I really need to stop doing this." I chuckled, taking a moment to press against Mark a little further rather than rush away in embarrassment.

My days of stumbling into Mark and being mortified because of it were long over. Admittedly, the move was rarely smooth and never planned, but it was kinda nice how he'd always been there to help right me. And that was the thing that I noticed the most between the two of us.

I didn't need catching, and it was nothing to do with the ten kilos I had on Mark and him not being able to do so; if I needed him to, he would. But, as we navigated through this climb, or in the past a hike, a damn aeroplane, and now our relationship, we were finding our balance. We could help each other stand

and find our equilibrium regardless of what we were doing. It was specifically that knowledge that had made me blurt out the fears I'd had last night.

And his answer hadn't been trying to shut me down or belittle my concerns either.

I swore he was bloody perfect, flaws and all.

"I'd prefer you not to," he said, and I leaned back a little so I could see his face better. "Any excuse to rub against you." He bobbed his eyebrows up and down, and I snorted.

I'd quickly learned that taking the piss was our version of foreplay, maybe even as close to romancing we'd get. And I was A-okay with that.

"Don't mind this pair," Frank said, startling me, but not enough to pull out of Mark's hold. We both glanced in his direction, seeing he was standing with Aiden, the new guy. Climbing wasn't the typical day for new members to try out, but it was clear Aiden could handle the ropes, certainly better than I could. "They're in the 'can't keep their hands off each other' stage." He shot us a shit-eating grin and followed up with a wink.

"Just letting you know I can't see this stage finishing anytime soon, Frank," I shot back, causing both

Frank and Mark to laugh, and I reluctantly put a small step between Mark and me, checking my carabiner, taking a quick look at the new guy. A tight smile was Aiden's only response.

I didn't have time to contemplate it as Frank added, "And so it begins." He raised his hand out before him in a "what are you going to do" gesture. "So, the reason I interrupted this lovefest, I wanted to introduce you to Aiden properly. He's just moved from Alice Springs, was actually in the founding charter of the Outback Boys there."

My eyes shot up at that. Aiden was a long way from home, and honestly, he didn't seem particularly happy about being here. I struggled to get a read on the guy.

"I imagine you regularly dealt with extreme conditions in the outback," Mark said. I smiled a little. Mark was so much better than I was at trying to break the ice. I imagined it was an essential part of his job—making people relax and building relationships.

"There were a few moments," Aiden responded, seeming to loosen up a little more. He still appeared on edge, maybe, but I wasn't sure that was what was a little off about the guy.

"And you've settled somewhere locally?" Mark asked as Frank excused himself, promising Aiden he'd only be a few minutes.

"Yeah, Eumundi at the moment. Just renting a place before I find a property."

"Oh, nice," I added. "Eumundi has a great feel to the town. Gets crazy during tourist season with the markets, but still a great place."

"Yeah." Aiden bobbed his head. "I noticed the extra cars and the building traffic on Wednesdays and Saturdays."

"Yeah. They're definitely the days to be staying home or heading out of town, for sure." I wanted to ask so much more, my curiosity rising to the surface, especially about the fact that he was looking for a property. I assumed he meant acreage or something, but I rarely pried. It was one of the things my gran had instilled in me as a kid—to never ask questions that were potentially awkward, difficult, or upsetting.

Honestly, I was grateful for her titbits of wisdom. So many times I'd stood by awkwardly as some nosey git had pried. And that was in all sorts of settings. Even here it happened, and especially when dealing with labels surrounding identity and sexuality, it was so easy to put your foot in it or make someone feel uncomfortable.

"Has Frank hooked you up with a climbing partner today?" Mark asked.

I wouldn't have known either way if Aiden had or not. Other than a brief greeting to the new guy at the beginning of the session and being aware I'd seen Aiden a little on the ropes, noticing he was good, my focus had been on not falling off the rock face and trying to keep my eyes off Mark's arse. The struggle was genuine, and I was happy as hell to have it—the latter specifically.

"Nah, not today. I'm just floating around. Getting a feel for the group." Aiden gave a small smile and glanced around at a couple of guys laughing loudly to the side. I grinned when I saw it was Pete and Muhammed. The friends had been in the group for longer than I had and were nice guys.

"Well, if you want a climb, I can spot you if you want?" Mark asked. "Trey just finished in spectacular style."

I snorted. "You mean by throwing myself at you?" As a big guy, my gracelessness was perhaps a little more obvious than if I'd been a few inches shorter and not quite so thickset. But the first was out of my control, and the latter I'd made peace with long ago. That I was a little firmer since being so active with Outback Boys was simply a bonus.

Mark laughed and reached out for me. I happily let him haul me close, not one to pass up on the affection. He pressed a kiss to my temple. "Stumbling is sexy," he said around a grin.

I rolled my eyes. "Yeah, let's go with that."

When I returned my attention to Aiden, he was observing the two of us. Unable to read his expression, I had no idea what he was thinking, but he smiled, possibly the first genuine one since meeting him. "If you don't mind, that'd be great, thanks," he finally said.

I edged back and undid my carabiner, okay to step back and pleased that Aiden seemed at ease enough to let down his guard a little and enjoy himself.

It didn't take long before he'd practically whizzed up the cliff face. The guy was fast and crazy fit. He'd barely broken a sweat. When Mark glanced over at me with his brows lifted high, I laughed.

"Right!" I said, not needing him to say a word.

"You sure you're not Spider-Man or some shit?" Mark called up at Aiden.

Aiden glanced down and chortled. "Not in this lifetime."

"Be extra careful where you put your hands, just in case," I hollered up. "A radioactive spider bite would morph you into something far crazier than Spider-Man with your existing mad skills."

Aiden snorted, and I grinned, stepping fully out of the way as Aiden made his descent down the rock face. In no time at all, he was before us, his smile wide. "Thanks for that. I didn't realise how much I needed it."

"Always happy to offer a helping hand, especially if it helps unwind," Mark said with a short head bob at Aiden. I watched the two interact, a shot of unease making its way into my chest.

Aiden was a good-looking guy, which was a mild way of saying he was incredibly hot. Not only was he tall, my sort of height, but he was a lot fitter than I was. He looked like he spent a lot of time outdoors, and while there was a seriousness about the man, Mark had brought a smile to his face a couple of times now.

Mark was equally sexy, and as far as I was concerned, I'd definitely dated up. Brown eyes met mine, drawing me out of my thoughts. My gaze dropped a little, zeroing in on Mark's mouth and roaming his face. The right side of his mouth kicked up, his whole focus seeming to be on me, capturing my attention so completely, my heartbeat picked up speed, and I was reminded just how good the past few weeks had been for the two of us.

A look was all it took to remind me that Mark wanted me.

My chest filled with air as I dragged in a breath and shoved away the tiny doubt and jealousy that had attempted to crawl on in.

There wasn't a chance I'd sabotage what we had.

We said goodbye to Aiden when he walked away with Frank, who seemed pleased we'd spent some time with the new bloke.

"Huh," Mark said when we were alone, wrapping one arm around my waist and putting his hand in my back pocket.

"What?"

"I could have sworn I saw a little… green or something on you a few moments ago."

I cocked my brow and dipped my gaze to make eye contact with him. "No idea what you're talking about."

He squeezed my butt, making me chuckle. "Either way, my hand is more than happy where it is."

"With a handful of arse?"

"Specifically your arse," he said, not missing a beat.

My lips quirked in amusement. That Mark had read me so well was fine by me, and the fact that he did just meant he was doing a bang-up job at getting to know me. It was this ability to cut through the BS that mattered, especially after my last shitshow of a relationship.

While my ex had taken big-time advantage with not paying his way, I'd discovered that lies flowed naturally from him, and he rarely said what he meant. And there wasn't a single moment when he could interpret a simple look from me so accurately. That would mean he'd have had to care enough to get to know me in the first place.

"So, I was meaning to invite you to an event happening in a few weeks." He looked a little shifty as he spoke—running his hand through his hair and sending a smile that looked like his offer wasn't all that great.

"Yeah?" I asked. "Is it something I need to be saying no to?"

Mark huffed out a laugh, dropping his eyes away as he helped me undo the straps of my belt. We'd had enough for the day, so we were packing up. While it was only late morning, the sun's rays were already touching the top of the rock face, and caught in the small valley meant the ground temperature was heating up something fierce. When my balls started to sweat, it was time to pack it in and seek out a shower.

"No, I definitely don't want you to say no." He finally finished unbuckling me and scooped up the ropes as I picked up the rest of our equipment. As we turned and headed towards the trail that would lead us back to his car, he said, "It is a black-tie charity event, though." My brows rose at that. I'd never been to one, and the closest I'd been to wearing a tux was a hand-me-down suit to my school formal years back and a hired suit to my sister's wedding a couple of years ago.

My curiosity piqued. "I get to see you dressed up in a tux?" The idea had absolute merit. I was already mulling over the closest bridal hire place that I'd be able to hire a tux from. I had no issue with seeing Mark all dressed up.

He cast me a small smile. "I can promise you I'll be wearing my tux."

It made sense he had his own. "So, what's the big deal?"

"It's for a really great charity," he said first.

"And?"

"It's something my mum started eighteen years ago. My grandad died of Alzheimer's when he was quite young. As soon as she had some pull and some funds, she went all gung-ho in this yearly event, raising funds."

I nodded. "That sounds amazing."

"It is, *she* is," he clarified. "Every year Mum raises a shitload and is so officious in making sure the money gets in the right hands, you know?"

I smiled. It was undoubtedly a good cause, and his mum sounded great for organising such an event. But that didn't explain his discomfort. Unless—

"Is it a problem me being there as your date?" A thought hit me. I widened my eyes. There was no way…. I kept my voice as controlled as possible, asking, "They know you date men, right?" I didn't wince and I didn't accuse, but I hoped like hell I'd got it wrong.

Mark's smile softened, and he lightly bumped his shoulder with mine, and I figured if both of our hands weren't full, he would have been holding my hand right about now. "I came out when I was in my last year at uni." I expelled my held breath as quietly as possible at that. "Mum's answer was research and trying to join me up to every LGBTQI+ organisation going and wanting to go with me to festivals. Dad's answer was insisting I picked up my taekwondo again, which I'd quit when I'd first left to go to uni."

"Really?" I shook my head in both amusement and confusion.

"Yeah. Dead set serious. In the trade, there's an equal amount of decent blokes compared to fuckwits. Dad knows me well enough to know that since I'd figured everything out and came out to them, I wouldn't be hiding my sexuality, and because of that, he wanted me to feel as safe as possible." Mark gave a casual shrug.

"Huh, that kinda makes sense. Sounds like a good guy."

"He is. Chilled out a bit more now he's semi-retired, not that he's anywhere near close enough to quitting just yet."

At the boot of his car, Mark reached out and opened it. I dumped our rucksack in it before taking some of the equipment off him that we took over to Frank's ute. Once we'd stored the equipment away, we waved goodbye to a couple of guys before climbing into Mark's vehicle.

It didn't take long for the icy blast of the air conditioning to push against my skin. Goosebumps trailed along my arms, and I sighed at the drop in temperature. "I didn't realise how bloody hot it was today."

"Right!" Mark nodded and glanced over at me. "You want to head out for lunch or back to mine?"

"I'm keen for a shower."

"Good plan." He pulled out of the car park, pressing the horn when he saw Frank. We both gave a small wave.

"I want to know more about taekwondo and knowing just how easily you can kick arse, but the charity event…." He still hadn't explained what the issue was, and I was sure there was one.

"They auction off special guests for dates." Mark sounded as disgruntled as he did resigned. Me? I snort laughed.

"You're shitting me?"

"I shit you not."

"And your fine self will be available for purchase?" I was entertained at the thought, but alongside was the niggle of awareness, wondering how much people paid for such a thing and how on earth I'd be able to afford him. While it was for charity, it didn't mean I liked the idea of him going on a date with someone else, innocent or not.

"Yeah, afraid so. Every year since I could legally drink."

I nodded, my brain working overtime, trying to figure out what to ask, and whether this was where his concern lay. Obviously he wanted me there, and I assumed it was as his boyfriend who'd also be bidding and winning him. "Is the date with a bloke or a woman?" Mark being gay and not sitting anywhere else on the rainbow flag meant that I'd feel more at ease if a woman won the date if I couldn't.

"Both bid. The dates aren't advertised as romantic, you know. In the past, I've been on dates with women for the charity, as well as guys."

I assumed not straight guys, but I could have got it wrong. "And don't dates being auctioned off have to be single?" Embarrassment hit my cheeks that I'd asked one of the questions swirling in my brain. Mark had referred to me as his boyfriend twice, and I'd done the same, so it wasn't that, but this seemed more official somehow, which didn't make a lick of sense.

"Engaged to be married or already wearing gold bands is the only definition of not single for the event."

"Okay, and you want me there…?" I deliberately lifted the sentence into a question when I trailed off.

"You need to save me and win."

CHAPTER TEN

MARK

W̲ORK HAD FINALLY CALMED DOWN A LITTLE. I'D PUT out the small fires threatening to spiral out of control and was even able to see Trey during the week these past three weeks. Each time I'd offered to head to his, or even just meet for dinner or something just out of the city, but every time he'd rejected the offer, reminding me he was happy to head the hour or so south to catch up with me.

Not only was I grateful that he saved me the journey, especially on days I'd been travelling to the Goldie, but having the opportunity to spend time with Trey during the week was something I could get used to.

When I'd left my apartment early this morning, I'd woken him with kisses to the neck, despite it only being just gone five. A couple of weeks back, he'd made it clear that he expected and wanted me to say goodbye to him rather than sneak out, not liking to wake alone.

I'd made the usual offer that he could set up in my office to work rather than race back to the Sunny Coast, but by that point, his face had been buried against my neck, his hand down my pants, and he was trying his hardest to drag me to bed to give me a definite answer.

Trey was hard to resist, so after not too much difficulty, we'd wrapped our hands around each other's cocks and had both come with gurgled grunts, his much sleepier than mine. Mornings when Trey was around were the best starts of my day, for sure.

"You're still wearing a shit-eating grin," Glen said, shaking his head at me. I was finishing up some emails, my office door open, before heading back to my apartment.

I snorted. "Am I?" I totally was, but my cousin didn't need a helping hand to take the piss.

He narrowed his eyes on me, though not enough to conceal the warmth there. "You are bringing this guy next weekend, right?"

I knew he meant the man putting a smile on my face. "Yeah, that's the plan."

His twitching mouth kicked up into a full smile. "Thank Christ for that. And you've prepared him for it, right?"

I winced a little at that. "Sort of."

Glen snorted. "If you really like the guy, which from how ridiculous you've been since getting back from America, I know the answer is yes, don't fuck this up. Let him know what to expect."

A ripple of anxiety ferreted its way into my gut. "You're making it sound like the charity gala is a shitshow."

He quirked his brow high at me. "Really? You seriously burying your head in the sand over this shit. Mate, this isn't the time to play dumb. You know as well as I do Keith will be there for one, and once he's had a few shots, his shitty slurs will come pouring out. Your mum's already threatened to castrate you if you deck him again."

Glen wasn't exaggerating. Keith was my sister's husband and was a fucking tool, a homophobic one at that. He kept his mouth shut, sensibly so, most of the time when in my or my parents' company, but once pissed, he didn't know when to shut up.

Every single time my poor sister was mortified, and try as we might, she refused to even consider divorcing him because she didn't want her kids to have a broken home. And that was despite the pleas of not only me but my parents as well. None of us had known what a shithead he was before they married. Keith had managed to keep a lid on his thoughts for two years of dating and being engaged.

I supported my sister as best as I could, doted on my one-year-old nephew, and I would my soon-to-be-born niece too.

"And…"

I knew what was coming, and I couldn't deny any of it. The whole thing really was a shitshow. I was crazy to be bringing Trey into the midst of it all.

"…I know Barry is going to be there."

"For definite?" It seemed keeping my head shoved up my arse was no longer an option. With my ex attending, I definitely had to tell Trey. We'd talked about our exes, Barry being my most recent, even though it was well over a year ago.

He hadn't liked me breaking up with him. It didn't help that he had a flair for the melodramatic, which I supposed was fitting since he was an actor. He'd starred in a few home-grown shows, had a bit of a name for himself, but simply put, he was a prick.

God only knew what Mum was thinking by inviting him. Though I supposed she just thought of the media he'd bring as well as the extra cash.

"Thought that would be enough to get the stars out of your eyes. Sorry, Mark, but man up and tell that boyfriend of yours what to expect."

My sigh was long and low. "Yeah, you're right. Make sure he sits next to you and April, though, yeah?"

"Only if I can dish the dirt." He waggled his brows ridiculously.

"As long as he's away from Keith and Barry, I don't give a shit."

He said goodbye, and I finished my email, dragging myself to the car to make my way home. I'd have to give Trey a call when I got back.

It was still light when I got to the apartment. The autumn sun, despite the early evening, hadn't cooled off much. The disgusting humidity didn't help the temperature much either. While I'd spent practically all afternoon in air conditioning, I'd still built up a sweat, especially as today I'd been trapped in a shirt and dress pants.

My shower was calling me, my need for food a close second, and then I'd have to call Trey and hope he wouldn't hightail it. I wouldn't blame him if he did. The evening sounded like a nightmare. Despite my mum's good intentions and the fundraising success I undoubtedly knew she'd have, depending on Trey's reaction, I would seriously consider letting my mum down.

I felt shit for even thinking it, but Trey was important to me, and I was tired of being put in situations time and time again to keep the peace. There were occasions it felt like I was the only one bending, and I was dangerously close to reaching my limit.

I yawned and rubbed my hand over my face as I stepped into the hallway of my apartment. Immediately I froze, removing my hand and tilting my head. The sound of metal, likely a pan being placed down, followed by the fridge's opening and closing drifted to me. I inhaled, the scent of something delicious cooking reaching my nostrils.

My smile was immediate.

I dumped my keys and phone on the small table in the hallway and took the few steps necessary to turn the corner and head into the open-plan kitchen area. My breath whooshed out of me, my shoulders relaxing, my heart flipping over itself when I took in Trey with his head in the fridge, arse sticking out, grumbling something to himself.

I leaned against the wall, enjoying the view and relishing in the knowledge that he'd stayed all day and was here cooking for me. But it was more than that. Coming home to Trey felt pretty fucking awesome. The whole apartment felt different, warmer and cosier somehow, just from Trey being in my space and treating the place as his own.

"Holy motherfucking shitballs." Trey'd stood, turned, and leaped a good two feet in the air, landing and grasping onto the fridge door with one hand while the other clutched his chest. "You really do need a bell." He shook his head and expelled a heavy breath. "I need to go and check my undies, fark my heart."

My laughter came quickly, lighting my chest and doing a bang-up job of pushing aside some of my previous anxiety. "I'll add a bell to my list," I joked, stepping towards him, my amusement subsiding, though my smile stretched wide. "You're still here," I said unnecessarily, but he *was* here, and I loved that he was.

Trey's mouth quickly morphed into a smile, no doubt reading my reaction easily since my grin was so wide. "Thought it would be nice to not rush off and to spend more time with you. That was okay, yeah?"

I was in his space in the next instant, but his hands reached me first, and Trey was the one hauling me close, his lips brushing across mine. When I pulled back, I said, "Yeah, of course. I love that you're still here. If I'd have known, I'd have finished up earlier and got back quicker."

Trey's lips quirked, but he shook his head. "That's why I didn't tell you. If you had to work, then you needed to be there and get stuff done. If you'd left earlier, you'd be chasing your arse tomorrow. I didn't want that."

Appreciation rippled through me. "Thanks," I said, and surprised myself by saying honestly, "I do want my hours to change, though. I can't keep it up. I need to be able to leave by five at the latest, you know?"

"I get it, especially if your day starts so early. I know you're knackered and want to get back so you can unwind." He stepped out of my hold, and I brushed past him to grab myself a beer, already spotting his open one on the counter.

"Yeah, there's that, but I want more of this." I removed the cap and leaned against the counter, Trey moving beside me, hip pressing against the granite edge and facing me.

"This as in…?"

"Spending time with you, not waiting for the occasional weekend to see each other. I know it's been a bit easier recently, which is great, but I don't want to be strategizing ways to find enough time to spend with you, you know?"

With his brows low, Trey looked extra kissable in his thinking state. Unable to resist, I pressed my mouth against his, encouraging him to open for me as I worked my lips against his. When he groaned softly, I reluctantly pulled away. There'd be time enough for me to suck him dry later.

After a beat, his frown lifted, and a smirk appeared on his face. "I'm rubbing off on you, huh?" I opened my mouth but was cut off when he said, "Nope, no rubbing off jokes."

I laughed, shrugging. "It's just there for the taking, though." Trey shook his head at me. "And yeah, you are. I want to spend more time with you." My words were out there, and I was sure my cheeks heated as I spoke. But Trey, being Trey, didn't tease me about my embarrassment or awkwardness—not when it came to shit like this.

"I miss you too," he said, understanding everything that I didn't say. "And do you have a plan on how to stop working fourteen-hour days?"

"Yeah," I answered, heading to the sink to wash my hands as the oven timer went off and Trey grabbed the oven gloves. "I'm meeting with Dad next week. I have some ideas." While they weren't fully formed plans just yet, I knew Dad would help me tighten up my proposal to make it work. Above anyone, he understood the demands of the position. While he'd managed everything pretty much by himself for so long, the company had grown significantly since I'd first stepped up to work with Dad, my initial job to expand our business.

I had and had done so well. But I couldn't let work be my all.

Washed up and food dished up, we sat on the sofa, the TV on low so we could continue to talk.

"If you want to talk through anything, I'm here. I may not understand the specifics of your company, but I should be able to keep up if you explain anything to me that I'm struggling with." Trey finished talking by putting slight pressure of his thigh against mine.

"Thanks, 'preciate it. As soon as I've got my thoughts together more, that'd be great."

A small smile lifted his lips, and I was pleased that not only did he want to support me, but that he was happy that I was willing to use him as a sounding board. I then cleared my throat, thinking about what my cousin and I had chatted about in the office. "So, while we're on the subject of talking through things, it's time for total disclosure about the charity event next weekend."

Trey seemed to brace himself as I started to explain all about my family dynamics—my wanker of a brother-in-law, who everyone but my sister detested; my ex who was a name and face he'd probably recognise, who was almost as much of a wanker as my brother-in-law, but for different reasons.

And by the end of it, while Trey looked a little shell-shocked, when he responded with "While you've your secret taekwondo moves, I've got my own arsenal to deal with bigots and dickheads, don't worry about me," I kissed him senseless and knew for sure that he was right. I needn't worry about Trey's ability to handle himself.

While he could be super quiet and reserved at times, there was a whole lot more to him that I'd yet to discover. And I couldn't wait to find out everything that made Trey tick.

CHAPTER ELEVEN

TREY

Bullshitting came naturally to me, apparently. In the days that whizzed by that led to me pulling on my collar and feeling a bit of a dickhead in my monkey suit, I'd convinced myself that everything was fine, and was sure I'd reassured Mark too.

"You look sexy as fuck," Mark said when we pulled up outside the hotel where the event was taking place. His voice and words were enough to distract me. I left my collar alone and glanced over at him.

"Thanks, I'll take it, but if that's what I am, not sure what that makes you." I was dead set serious. His tux, which was his own, fitted him to perfection. He scrubbed up incredibly. Not only was he a man of many talents, he looked good doing anything and everything.

His answer was to throw me a grin and angle over to me, a clear invitation. Willingly, I leaned over the console and pressed my mouth to his. It was chaste for us. Every time I even felt his breath caress my skin, I couldn't resist the man, and I was more than okay with that. Just last week, when I'd been due to stay for a night, it had ended up being four before I had to head back north for a client meeting.

Being together was easy, and I reminded myself of that as we pulled our mouths apart. Tonight could possibly be interesting, just as it could be fun or a shitshow. Either way, I'd be going home with Mark.

"Ready?"

I nodded, reminding my racing heart I could handle bullshitting myself and Mark's family if needed tonight. I willed myself to take deep, even breaths. "Yeah, all good."

Mark's gaze searched mine, and he offered me a wink before he opened the door, a guy on the other side pulling it fully open for him as another valet did the same with my door once I'd opened it a crack. As I turned, Mark's voice had me pausing and looking in his direction.

Both of his feet were outside the car. Bent over, he leaned his head through the open door. "You asked what that makes me."

Confused for a beat, my brows dropped low until I recalled me struggling to describe his level of hotness. I quirked a brow, amused and curious. "And?"

"Yours," he said. "It makes me yours."

My thoughts screeched to a halt before speeding back up again, moving so quickly it was difficult to do anything beyond breathe, and even that was an effort.

"Sir."

The voice of the valet snagged my attention, and I remembered I needed to get out of the car. I did so with an expression that I was sure made me look like I was deranged, or ill, or who the hell knew what. I said thanks, and my gaze found Mark. Waiting for me at the bottom of the staircase, he quirked the right side of his mouth high, and while his eyes were soft, tender even, the bastard knew what he'd been doing. His amusement was plain to see.

"Really?" My tongue flicked at the back of my teeth, my jaw tight as I battled with my disbelief and the laughter trying to escape. I reached his side, and he took my hand in his, the gesture doing nothing to settle my heavily beating heart or the butterflies that had taken flight in my gut.

His mouth stretched into a grin, and Mark lifted one shoulder in a carefree shrug.

"You owe me for that." He seriously did. Throwing such sentimental words my way, ones that were all sweet and swoon-worthy and shit, *now*, when there was nothing I could do about it…. Yeah, he'd be making it up to me.

"I do?" he asked, his face the picture of innocence. "I was just giving you incentive to win a date with me." He squeezed my hand as we made it up the stairs. Just before we entered, he said quietly, "Don't forget to let me know if you need to escape. I'll make it happen."

I snorted and glanced over at him, only to see he was serious. That sobered me up pretty fast. He'd warned me about the people that I needed to be warned or prepared for. He'd even given me a breakdown of a few key players, and honestly, his brother-in-law and his ex were not on my radar at all. I could deal with arseholes, and Barry sounded like a dickhead and was an ex for a reason.

Then there were his parents. They sounded great, but fuck, I was nervous. It was a big deal being here with Mark, making a statement to his family that we were dating and serious enough for me to be meeting them.

And while I believed Mark that they were good people and I'd be fine, it didn't make a lick of difference. I wanted to make a good impression, wanted them to like me.

With that thought, I checked that I was armed with my ability to bullshit, should I need to use it, and we walked into the buzzing room of black tuxes and colourful dresses.

The first thing obvious to me an hour into the event was that his dad liked a beer, thought people dressing up was a pain in the arse, and that he could take the piss out of people while flipping the switch fast and fierce when he needed to be professional. That, and he doted on his family.

Well, everyone except his son-in-law, Keith.

The dynamics, especially since we were in public and a formal setting, were bizarre. Melvin, Mark's dad, simply ignored the very existence of his son-in-law, and all without giving a rat's arse or making a big deal of it. The whole thing was impressive, really.

Whenever Keith said anything even remotely in Melvin's direction, Mark's dad deflected by talking to someone else, looking the other way. It was crazy awkward, but after an hour of seeing Keith necking whisky like it was water and getting louder, I thought Melvin deserved a damn medal for being in the same room as the guy.

Ellen, Mark's sister, was a quandary. An hour didn't give me much to go on, but the strain around her eyes was apparent, and she was terrific at smoothing over the obvious slights against her husband. Plus she seemed genuinely lovely.

Family dynamics were a hell of a thing, and absorbing the strange tension in the Hutchings family was an excellent distraction for the night, mainly because I didn't feel on show.

Linda reached out and placed her hand on my forearm as we took our seats, the auction about to begin. Mark's mum was precisely how he'd described her. Within two minutes, I'd liked her. She'd hugged me, all but slapping my hand away when I'd held it out to shake, and immediately put me at ease before she'd disappeared doing her hostess duties. But for the main event, she was here at the centre table.

"Did Mark talk to you about Barry?" Open, honest eyes stared back at me in the dim light, the battery candles flickering on our table casting her face in shadow.

Surprised by her question, I nodded, not saying anything.

"Good. Has he set you up?"

My surprise morphed into confusion. "Set me up?"

"To bid," she clarified.

I grinned. "Yeah. Mark sort of indicated that he wanted that date with me."

She bobbed her head. "That's good. Barry's such a prick," she said, making me chuckle. "Last year the slippery shit managed to outbid everyone."

My brows rose. Mark hadn't told me that, no doubt a memory he'd wanted to bury. Not yet having met Barry, I couldn't judge for myself, but everything I'd heard told me enough, and I was in no hurry to run into him.

"It was ridiculous. Don't get me wrong, great for the charity, but still, I know Mark would be pissed if he managed to win."

A flush of nerves rippled through me the more she spoke, wondering just how high he'd bid. Why the hell hadn't I asked Mark how much I could expect to pay? Like a fool, the one time he'd brought up money, I'd brushed him aside. Truth was I'd been a little indignant that he thought it was something for me to worry about.

Sure he was wealthy, but I wasn't a pauper, and this wasn't a big A-list event or anything. For real, we were in Brisbane, not LA or something.

"I think he broke the record for the highest bid," she continued, adding a roll of her eyes for good measure. "I wish like hell he didn't have to be invited, but sometimes social politics get in the way." She wrinkled her nose at that. "But if you're all set, maybe he'll finally realise Mark isn't interested, and he has a lovely boyfriend looking out for him."

Linda's words warmed me, easing some of my anxiety that she seemed to be rooting for her son and me. The warmth quickly froze over, turning to ice as rapidly as liquid nitrogen being poured over me when she said, "But still, the extra twenty-seven thousand dollars was a brilliant boon, I suppose."

She carried on talking, but I was stuck on twenty-seven thousand dollars. White noise filled my ears and vibrated around my head. How on earth could I afford that much cash? Perhaps I hadn't heard right, but before I could ask for clarification, the emcee started the evening with an introduction and an explanation of the auction.

I was mildly aware of clapping, merely following the lead of those on my table. I heard figures of money being thrown around, ones much closer to what I'd been expecting, for the first few men being auctioned off. The highest being five thousand made me wince, but my credit card would cover that.

But twenty-seven thousand?

What the fuck was I going to do?

"You doing all right over here?"

I turned at the quiet voice. It was Glen, one of Mark's cousins who I'd been introduced to tonight. From the few moments we'd spent chatting and from his obvious distaste of Keith, he seemed like a good guy, and Mark had vouched for him before we'd arrived.

"Yeah, sure," I said noncommittedly. My smile was tight and not exactly reassuring, too focussed on the calculations going on in my head.

Glen snorted. With his voice still low, he said, "You sure about that? You look a bit freaked by whatever Aunt Linda said earlier."

I sighed, figuring to hell with it when I asked, "Just how pissed will Mark be if I don't win?"

His brows shot high before dipping low. "You're not planning on bidding?"

"It's not that."

For a few beats, he remained quiet. When his brows evened out, he answered, "Well, if his ex wins, he won't be happy, but Mark'll suck it up." His lips pursed closed, his gaze roaming my face before he said, "Didn't Mark fix you up with the funds to make sure you won?"

There was no holding back my wince when I admitted, "I may have shut him down, thinking it wouldn't cost so much I couldn't afford the bid." Embarrassment flushed through me, and I was grateful we were in the low-lit room.

"Ah, gotcha. Aunt Linda told you the price he went for last year, huh?"

I nodded and huffed out a breath, relieved that Glen genuinely did seem like a good bloke and wasn't making me feel like an idiot.

"Want my advice, mate?"

Since I had no ideas of my own, I was more than happy to listen to any he may have. "Go for it."

"Win the auction and let my cousin pay. It's no big deal."

The problem was it felt like one.

Glen must have read something into my expression as he said, "Seriously, just do it and don't sweat it. He brought his friend Jules a few years back, just to piss off his mum I think, and made sure he covered the bid. Last year just took him by surprise, as he didn't realise until too late that Barry was here."

I bobbed my head and attempted a smile. "Okay, thanks."

Glen looked over his shoulder before saying, "Listen, the wife wants me, so I've gotta go slip back in my seat. Mark's up soon, so get ready."

Absently, I said goodbye, my mind too focused on this ridiculous bid. The reality was I couldn't afford a bucketload of cash to give to charity, and Mark could. I expected if I hadn't cut Mark off when he'd tried to discuss the auction with me, he would have offered anyway, preventing me from feeling mortified.

It pissed me off that I felt that way, but there was nothing I could do about it other than swallow my pride or go for broke. Though in the back of my mind, I continued to calculate all of my funds. There was a possibility, but it was cutting it fine. The alternative was letting Mark suck it up with his ex, which sounded wrong on every single level. So, yeah, that wasn't going to happen.

The emcee's voice cut through my thoughts when he introduced Mark. Immediately my gaze zeroed in on him, the man who'd already flipped me upside down earlier by saying he was mine. He looked incredible under the bright spotlight, and combined with the small smirk he offered the audience, as far as I was concerned, he was the hottest person here tonight.

Mark's eyes flashed around the crowded tables, settling on me before he offered a wink.

My grin was instant.

The overconfident arsehole was mine, dammit, and so what if winning this date changed things a little. Maybe next year, there wouldn't be a chance of his mum forcing him to participate. The thrill of the possibility of the two of us being in a very different place this time next year raced through my stomach.

"We're going to start this evening's bid at three thousand dollars."

I subtly watched the room, spotting numbered boards shoot in the air. Panic shot through me. I didn't have a paddle. I glanced around the table, wondering if there was one around. Was it something I should have organised beforehand? Shit, I was so screw—

"Here, Trey, I imagine you'll be needing this." Linda passed me the board, a broad smile on her face as she threw me a wink, not so unlike her son's.

"Thank you," I whispered, turning back to the bidding war going on. Already we were at twenty-two thousand. My attention moved to the arsehole ex, who Glen had pointed out earlier. As soon as he had, I'd recognised Barry's face.

The man was sitting bolt upright, his gaze determined.

There wasn't a chance in hell he was going to win.

There was an elderly lady bidding, but she hesitated over her last bid. It was clear she'd be backing down.

"Twenty-eight thousand dollars is the final bid. Going once…"

Nerves hit my stomach. I didn't want this to go in a bidding war.

"…going twice…"

I needed to shut this shit down.

"Forty thousand, five hundred and seventy-two dollars," I hollered, paddle in the air, absolute determination in my voice. I shot a glance at Barry, who faced me, his brows high, his mouth gaping wide. *Take that, dickhead.*

"And forty thousand, five hundred and seventy-two dollars," the emcee said, amusement in his voice, "if there are no advances, going once, going twice, and sold to the gentleman, number 179." The gavel followed immediately after, and my breath whooshed out of me.

Loud shouts from our table had me laughing and glancing around. I bypassed Keith's look of repulsion and concentrated on Linda's wide smile, Melvin's grin and nod of approval, and Glen's smirk and thumbs up.

I was mildly aware of the emcee wrapping things up, but I didn't even have time to turn and look before strong hands appeared on my shoulders and warm breath swept close to my ear.

"You are fucking incredible." Mark's words were warm and quiet. I angled around to see his face so close to mine. Heat reflected in the depths of his eyes, and he wore the biggest grin I'd seen him with yet. My heart flipped over at his reaction.

I didn't get the chance to respond, though, before his mouth was on mine. The kiss was chaste and sweet, him more than me remembering his parents were less than a metre away from us. He pulled back, his gaze roaming mine. "You ready to get out of here?"

"I—"

"I don't bloody think so, Mark." Linda's voice cut through my response. We both looked at her. Her lips twitched with amusement.

"Mum...."

Mark's whine had me snorting, enjoying that it didn't matter a man's age or success, he was still able to be put in his place by his parents and took on the same tone I imagined he used when he was a teenager.

"Just thirty minutes, then you can get your butts out of here, okay?" She took on the whole mum-voice tone and look, which had Mark agreeing.

With a childish huff from Mark that kept my smirk in place, he sat in the empty chair beside me, pulling it close so he could hold my hand.

Not long after, the lights brightened a little as desserts were brought out. I was enjoying the dark chocolate torte when Keith's question had me looking up.

"What is it you do again to afford, what was it, forty thousand, five hundred and seventy-two dollars? That's a ridiculously specific number."

I finished chewing and answered, as politely as I could, "I'm a web developer."

"Didn't realise that paid so much that you'd be flush with cash," he said, the slightest of slurs in his voice.

"Keith, how's your dessert?" Ellen said. "Would you like to try some of mine?"

Keith didn't even look at Mark's sister when he said, "No." Instead, his eyes were fixed on me. "Huh, okay, I get it now." A sly smirk appeared on his face, and he glanced over at Mark. "Didn't think you had it in you, Marky boy. Just wondering whether rent boys charge by the minute or the hour these days."

"The fuck you say?" Mark spat. I clamped on his arm as he made to stand. Taut muscles constricted under my grip.

"Keith, really," Linda said, "I think it's about time you finished your drink and got Ellen home. Unless you'd like to come home with us, Ellen?" she said, directing her question at her daughter. The concern was apparent in her voice, making my gut twist at the strangeness of having Keith in this family.

"She'll be coming home with me, Linda," Keith said, surprisingly cordially. "Didn't mean to insult Mark's choices." His lip curled as he looked in our direction, making it very clear that was precisely his intention.

Me? I laughed. The sound deep and loud, and yeah, a little forced, but fuck this guy.

"Something funny?" Keith asked, his confusion laced with obvious distaste.

"Not especially," I answered, wondering why this guy thought he could get away with the shit he did. While I didn't have a physical job, I was a big guy, and I wasn't as soft around the middle as I used to be. While perhaps I didn't have the same presence as Mark, who commanded a room with ease, my size alone was enough to make people—usually guys who were being pricks—hesitate. "I don't know if I'm flattered or insulted that you think I'm, what, good-looking enough to hire out my services? That I've caught your attention enough to think someone like Mark would pay for a piece... well, damn, I think I quite like the idea."

Red swept across Keith's face, fast and blazing. He gaped a moment before fumbling his words, saying, "That's not what I— I didn't think— You're not fuc—"

"No, no, it's okay." I cut him off, more than aware of Mark's grip tightening on my hand. "Thanks for thinking I'm hot enough to be eye candy. Clearly all of my outdoor—" Could I say the next part with his parents at the table? I hesitated barely a second before just going for it. "—and *inside* activities with Mark are paying off."

A strangled sound came from somewhere deep in Mark's throat, but I didn't look away from Keith, taking a sadistic kind of delight at his discomfort. "And don't worry about my finances. I have enough in savings to cover the *very* specific amount." And I did, at a push. I'd been saving for a house for a while now. Between that and my credit card, I'd calculated how much I could afford to close the bid down. Not that I could dwell on that for too long, as the thought made me feel sick.

"Okay, now that's settled," Linda intervened, casting a friendly smile my way. "Your thirty minutes have sped on by. Why don't you go and settle up your payment, and you crazy kids get out of here?" Considering it had been barely five minutes, Linda was giving us an out both Mark and I were happy to take, with how quickly both of us stood.

I kissed his mum's cheek and did the same to Ellen, as well as Glen's wife. When it came to saying goodbye to Melvin, he surprised me by catching me in a firm hug, patting my back. "Make sure you both come for a barbie the next time the cricket's on," he said.

I nodded, more than happy to do that, despite not being a big fan of cricket. "Will do. Thanks."

I shook Glen's hand, and he smirked widely. "Next time you're down, get Mark to let me know, and you can drop by or something," he said, "meet the horde." Once more, I agreed, and then in the next breath, Mark was tugging me away.

Before we got to the counter to pay, Mark stopped me, pulling me to the side for some privacy. "You know I want to suck you off so bad, right?"

A laugh burst free of me just as quickly as my dick twinged when I thought about his hot mouth. "I hate to stand in the way of your plans."

He groaned, pressing his lips to mine, once again the kiss chaste and doing nothing to quench my need to taste him. "You go and grab the car, and I'll settle up." He handed me the ticket.

I took it, saying, "I do have that money, so can pay."

Intensity filled his eyes. "I know, and it means a lot you'd pay it. Thank you. But you're my date. You've saved my arse. So you're good for me to pay, yeah?"

My breath whooshed out of me. "Thank fuck for that," I admitted with a laugh. "I'd be renting for another ten years if not." Mark raised his hand and cupped my cheek, a move he only made when he was all tender and shit. "Thank you." I leaned into the comfort of his palm, not caring we were still in public, not caring the both of us were being sappy.

"That's where the money was coming from? Saving for a house."

I bobbed my head and gave a one-shoulder shrug. "Kinda think you're worth it."

Mark grinned at my words. "I kinda think you're worth it too." Then our mouths connected, this time a little deeper, a little hotter, complete with a quick sweep of my tongue against his. When he pulled away, he licked his bottom lip and swallowed. "Car. Meet you in two."

I nodded and walked away, shooting his ex a megawatt grin when he stood to the side, mouth open wide and looking like he wasn't quite sure what to do with himself. I was more than okay with that. There's been no drama, no fuss, and I'd made my intentions perfectly clear. And that hot kiss Mark and I had just shared? Yeah, the statement was loud and clear.

Mark was mine, just as I was his. And we had no plans to be changing that fact anytime soon. Or maybe even ever if things carried on the way they were.

A man could hope.

CHAPTER TWELVE

MARK

"How'd it go?" Trey angled to look at me. He was on the sofa situated to take full advantage of the views of the sparkling ocean.

It was a clear autumn day, and while we edged closer to winter, it remained warm, some days peaking to hot. Trey looked at home on the sofa, his laptop on the small table beside him. I hoped he hadn't worked there all day. His back would kill him if he had. I'd offered to put a desk in front of the window, knowing he loved looking out at the beach when he spent time working here, but he wouldn't hear it, refusing to move anything around for him.

I planned to change that as soon as possible.

"Good," I said, a broad grin forming on my lips as I stepped closer. I leaned down and dotted a kiss on his welcoming mouth, sighing into the contact and wondering how I'd managed for so long without receiving kisses from Trey so regularly.

When I pulled back, his eyes were wide, and he stared at me intently. I snorted a laugh. "What?"

Trey shook his head. "You can't stop at good." I could practically feel the buzz of anticipation rolling off him. I got it. This last meeting was a big deal for me, for us.

It had taken weeks of discussion with my dad and a shitload of planning, but at this last meeting we'd agreed on the final details and signed the particulars.

"Let me grab a beer, and we'll sit on the balcony."

He nodded and stood, making his way to the kitchen to get the drinks while I toed off my shoes and tugged my shirt off, grabbing a tee from the folded laundry in the basket I'd dumped there last night and still hadn't bothered to move.

After pulling it on, I followed Trey outside. Inhaling deeply, I paused, soaking in the moment, the peace and rightness of it all. Trey spent more and more time in the city with me during the week, only staying away if he had client meetings, but with the vast majority of his work remote, it made it possible to be pretty much wherever he wished. I was just happy he'd decided that place was with me as often as he could. And at the moment, we were back at the Sunny Coast since I met Dad at my parents' house.

Over the past few weeks, I'd done a better job at delegating, finally realising that I couldn't run things the way Dad once had. The company was too big, the demands too much for me to do so. And after a run of meetings with Dad, he'd recognised the fact as well.

"So, spill," Trey said, his laser-focus gaze on me.

"It's done," I said, my smile big and a huge exhale tearing from me. "Glen signed the paperwork as a new company director. He's happy with the final package offered, and we've signed off on the site in Buderim for the new office." Just the thought of the changes and knowing that in nine months or so I'd be able to give up my apartment in New Farm sent a jolt of contentment through me. Brisbane's main office would remain open, with my cousin based there, but I'd be moving to the Sunshine Coast permanently. Being close to the airport helped for trips to Sydney or Melbourne when needed; anything else, and I could handle the slightly longer journey, knowing I didn't carry the running of the company by myself.

"That's brilliant. I'm happy for you." Trey's smile was bright and genuine. I matched it, already feeling some of the heavy tension ease off me. The Sunny Coast was my home; it was where I was the happiest. Not only that, Trey was here.

"Thanks. I think you gave me the final push I needed."

Trey's brows jerked high. "What do you mean?"

"I would have just kept sucking it up, kept going if you hadn't stumbled and made your move. You made me realise I wanted more."

A light blush crept across his cheeks. "Yeah?"

"Definitely," I said, meaning my words completely.

He seemed to take that in, his gaze roaming my face. After a beat, he swallowed loudly, the sound making me wonder what was on his mind. I didn't have to wait long before his words startled the hell out of me.

"So, my lease runs out on my apartment in six weeks. I've got two weeks left to give my notice or re-sign."

A shot of nervous excitement raced through me. Rather than pouncing on the implication of Trey's words—and him—and begging the man to give notice and move in with me tomorrow, let alone wait six weeks, I nodded, indicating I'd heard what he said and was listening.

Trey studied me before saying, "So I was thinking, if we're ready, we could look at moving in together or something. I already spend a good five nights a week with you." He cleared his throat, heat flushing his cheeks and his eyes alight with uncertainty. "What do you think?"

"I think we should start moving you in tomorrow," I said quickly, making him laugh as I scooted over and straddled him, needing his mouth on mine.

"Yeah?"

"Definitely yeah. I'm serious about tomorrow or whenever, though," I said between pressing kisses to Trey's mouth and then trailing them down his neck. He grabbed my arse and tugged my hips closer. We both grunted at the friction. "I'm still in the city for a while. We can continue with you coming out there when you can, but spending every night with you, or as many as I can get, I'm down with that."

I kissed my way back up his neck, returning to his mouth and capturing his lips in a tender kiss, not quite ready to get my cock too worked up. When I pulled back, it was to look down at Trey. Tenderness shone in his eyes, and I liked seeing it directed my way a hell of a lot.

"So I suppose this is the part where I tell you that I love you, right?"

I snorted despite the way my heart pulsed with a rush of adrenalin and beat faster at his declaration. It didn't matter how blasé he attempted to say the words. I had no doubt he felt them soul-deep, just like I did. "You can tell me that whenever you want as long as you follow up with your mouth on mine."

The right side of his mouth lifted into a smile. "Is that right?" he asked, his tone turning playful.

"Yeah, I reckon so, as long as you don't mind me telling you I love you whenever the mood takes me."

Trey huffed out a deep laugh, the sound vibrating through. "That sounds like a good plan to me."

Before I could get my mouth on his, my phone rang. I sighed, considering ignoring it, but I thought better and lifted up a little to tug it from my pocket. Mum's name was lit up on the screen.

"Hey, Mum."

"She's finally done it," she said by way of greeting.

My thoughts immediately went to Ellen. "The baby, what, she's not due quite yet, right?"

"No," she said, a mixture of exasperation and barely contained glee in her voice. "Keith, she found out he was having an affair. I was the straw. You know the battle it's been for her, especially with his overall behaviour."

"The fucker." At my words, Trey gripped my hips. When I saw his concern, I pulled the phone away, putting Mum on speaker. "Trey's here. He can hear you."

"Hey, honey," she said shortly before continuing, "Don't even get me started. The nerve of the man. Your dad's going berserk. Your poor sister is morti-fied but seems more pissed off than devastated, which is a good thing, right?"

I huffed out a breath. Anger battled with my relief for my sister, the two reactions coming together tricky to get a grip of. "I suppose, but make sure you don't just go bull at a gate, tearing Keith to shreds. Just make sure you say and do what Ellen needs you to do, yeah?" Even though we all hated the man, my sister must have loved him at some point, I was sure. I just really hoped she still didn't. Her relationship was something she refused to discuss with me. But maybe now it would be different.

"I know, I know. But she's already kicked him out. Literally thrown his things out the window and door onto the front lawn. She's asked me to not go around yet, but I'll call her again to make sure she's okay." Mum's glee turned to sorrow. "She'll be okay, won't she?"

I nodded, pain for my sister slamming into my chest. Trey gave my waist another squeeze, drawing my gaze to his and offering me a supportive smile.

"She'll be fine, Mum. She's got us, right?"

An exhausted sigh slipped past Mum's lips, travelling heavily down the line. "True. Your dad said everything's sorted with Glen," she said, changing the subject.

My mouth curved into a small smile. "It sure has been."

"I'm happy for you, Mark. I think it's a really good decision. Plus I get to see you more often, right?"

I snorted out a laugh. "Right." My parents weren't too demanding, and the truth was I liked spending time with them. And my sister's change in situation seemed even more significant of the developments to come. Assuming she divorced Keith, she'd be raising my niece and nephew by herself. Keith was a waste of space as a dad already, so there wouldn't be a custody battle. I was confident about that.

"Anyhow, call your sister in the morning. Maybe just text her tonight."

"Will do, Mum."

We said our goodbyes and ended the call. The elation from just a few moments ago had completely vanished. With a sigh, I climbed off Trey and moved to his side, staring out at the rolling waves, breathing in the fresh air, and trying to let its calming presence do its job.

"What happened?" he asked quietly.

"An affair, but I don't know any more."

"From your reactions, I'd figured. Shit, that sucks, man. Keith's a real piece of shit, huh?"

"For sure."

Trey leaned into me. "Sorry that your family's hurting."

I smiled at that. "I feel shitty that I'm happy that he's out of the family, or will be officially before long, away from my sister, you know. Ellen must be feeling… I don't know, shit, angry?"

"A whole lot of things, I'd imagine."

"It's kind of taken the celebration out of me," I admitted, feeling defeated.

"I get it." Trey went quiet for a few beats before he reached out and took my hand, saying, "Why don't you text Ellen and see if she wants to chat or wants you to go and visit. If she doesn't, I can run that huge tub of yours. We've still yet to christen it. We can chill, drink beer, and if you promise not to drown me, I'll even suck you off." He wiggled his brows up and down. Laughter rushed out of me. I was grateful as hell for the day Trey walked into my life.

"Okay, I can do that for sure. Just don't add bubbles or anything. I want nice clear water so I can see all the action."

He leaned in for a kiss, pulling away, saying, "That I can do."

He stood as I looked at my phone, opening my messenger app. Before I typed out my message to Ellen, I glanced over at Trey and smiled even though he couldn't see it. "Trey," I called out before he entered our bedroom. It felt really damn good to think of it that way.

"Yeah?" he asked, turning slightly and directing his whole focus on me.

"Thanks."

His brows pulled together. "What for?"

My gaze didn't waver, and my voice didn't tremble as I said honestly, "For letting me be yours."

Emotion filled his eyes when he stared back at me, his mouth tight, and I got it. I swallowed a ridiculous-sized lump as soon as I'd said the words.

It took a beat for his features to relax and for him to say, "Change of plan. Send the text and get your arse on the bed. You've got one minute before I drag you in there."

He strode out, clearly on a mission, my laughter chasing after him.

Sometimes plans changed, for good or bad, but either way, I'd learned to roll with each one the best I could.

But this one, knowing Trey needed me as much as I did him, those were the times that I'd move heaven and earth if necessary to remind him time and time again that I *was* absolutely his.

I'D FELT WEIRD LETTING MARK BUY ME A TUX, BUT HE was generous and ridiculously hard-headed when he was on a mission. But standing in front of the full-length mirror wearing the sleek black tux the fit me to perfection, I was no longer grumbling.

"You look hot."

I flashed a glance in the mirror to see Mark in the open doorway of the bathroom. I shot him a grin. "Yeah?" I preened a little, more than happy to receive a compliment from the man who made my pulse race.

"Make that a hell yeah and you'll get close to just how hot you look."

I turned to face him, watching his long legs eat up the distance between us. A moment later, he pressed his body against me and dotted a kiss to my neck. I used the moment to inhale his scent, loving that he wore the aftershave I'd bought him for his birthday. It was sweet and spicy, but still had that masculine hint to it that suited him perfectly.

"You smell delicious," I said with a sigh, as he planted a second kiss, this time behind the sensitive space behind my ear. "And if you keep doing that, I'm more than happy to let you strip me off. We can just make a donation another way, right?"

He snickered against my neck as he pulled away. "You seriously want to piss my mum off?"

I blanched. "Err, no thanks." His mum was incredible, but there was no chance I wanted to get on the wrong side of her.

"Come on then. Arse into gear." His palms squeezed said arse, which did nothing to help my desire to leave our bedroom and go to the charity gala.

"Fine. And are you sure you have to be on offer again?" I would have attempted a pout if I would have thought it would have had any impact on Mark other than a snort and a smirk, but I had to try. This year, however, I was prepared.

Once we'd moved into Mark's awesome house, it meant that cash certainly wasn't as tight. I contributed to the household stuff, but since Mark was mortgage free, for the first time ever, I had extra funds, meaning I saved a lot. Though, if the bid got ridiculously high, I had no hesitation in drawing funds from my boyfriend. Any pent-up issues I had about that were long gone. And it was nice, hell, perfect even.

But this auction I hoped would be the last where he'd be available. This time last year Mark had told me engaged or married were the only exceptions made to participating in the charity event, which had been firmly on my mind the last few weeks.

"Come on." Mark's hand tugging mine pulled me from my thoughts and away from the mirror.

"Fine. Let's get to it."

"That's the spirit." He flicked me a wink as he released my hand.

"I'll meet you by the door. Just need to grab my wallet," I said quickly once we were in the hallway. He bobbed his head and I retreated into our bedroom and the walk-in closet. Before I opened my undies' drawer, I tilted my head to the side to listen. With Mark still in the hallway, I tugged it open and ferreted around until I clasped the small leather box.

My heart rate spiked on contact, and as I pulled it out, taking a quick peek at the platinum and carbon fibre band, complete with small black diamonds, a smile tugged at my lips.

"You got it?" Mark called out.

I shoved the box into my pants pocket and took a deep breath. Nerves buzzed through me, anticipation fluttering in my stomach something fierce. With a second fortifying breath, I headed out of the closet and directly towards the man who I hoped like hell would agree to be mine forever by the end of the night.

———

THIS TIME SETTLING DOWN AT OUR ASSIGNED TABLE WAS a lot less effortless than last year. All of Mark's family greeted me with a hug, Ellen giving my hand a tight squeeze, a twinkle in her eyes when she said, "All prepared?"

I nodded, my smile coming quickly. She was the only person in on my plans. Over the past year she'd been through a lot, mainly with her divorce and settling into a new norm, but it was over the past six months especially, that we'd spent more time with each other. And I liked her a lot.

I'd quickly discovered she had the best dirt on the man in my life and provided me with plenty of ammo that would get Mark quickly kissing me into silence.

"You okay?"

Mark's quiet question next to my ear caught me by surprise. I'd been gazing around the room, honestly, looking to see if his smarmy ex was here rather than admiring the decorations.

"Yeah, sure." I glanced over and up at him, not having realised he was standing. "Going somewhere?"

A grimace appeared on his face. "Mum said there's a problem or something. I've just got to check out what the issue is, see if she needs anything."

"Need a hand?" I made to stand, but his palm on my shoulder kept me seated.

"Honestly, it's fine. I'll see what it is and then let you know. Thanks, baby." He tilted down and pressed his mouth against mine while I melted a little more inside. When he was like this, so damn sweet and looking as sexy as he did in his tux, it was hard to concentrate on anything but him. I was also so bloody tempted to tug my ring out of my pocket right this second, as him looking at me this way, made this one of hundreds of perfect moments.

"Okay. Give me a yell if you need me."

My words won me another light kiss before I watched him walk away, my gaze zeroing in on his shoulders and then his arse. The man seriously knew how to wear a tux.

"You've got drool." Ellen's words were full of sass, and as I glanced at her and matched her wide smile with my own, I threw her a wink.

"Only 'cause I want to take a bite out of his arse," I shot back, then widened my eyes immediately, realizing I wasn't being exactly quiet.

Ellen snorted and Melvin's booming laughter joined in. Embarrassment slammed into me as I looked at Mark's dad.

"Uhm, I mean…." I had nothing. There was no correcting or saving that.

"We Hutchings men are known for our firm back-sides," he said with a wide grin.

"Ewww," Ellen added while I shifted a little awkwardly.

"Not sure Linda's ever said mine's biteable. I'll ask her when she comes back."

Ellen groaned. "God, Dad, please don't do that." She swiped up her glass of champagne and necked it. "Trey, fill me up. You need to be responsible for getting me blotto since you're responsible for images of my dad's and brother's arses." She scrunched up her face in disgust.

I laughed, offering her a shrug. "But your dad's not wrong."

"Stop!" She sent me a death glare and held her glass steady while I topped her up.

Just as I finished filling up her glass, Linda and Mark returned, both smiling, and Mark looking like a cat that had got the cream with the grin spread across his mouth.

My brows jumped high. "No problem then?"

He shook his head and planted a big kiss on my mouth, the smile still on his face. "Nope," he said, pulling away.

My brows furrowed in confusion. "So what's with the crazy grin?"

He shrugged, but there was nothing nonchalant about it. He was all but vibrating.

I narrowed my eyes, about to question him more when Linda saying my name drew my attention to her.

"Thank you so much, Trey. You're such a good sport for doing this."

My brows dipped low. "Huh? What?" I shook my head, and glanced at Linda, then at Mark. Mark's grin looked painful it was so damn big and my stomach somersaulted. "What did you do?"

"Mark." Linda said her son's name on a disgruntled sigh. "Did you really not ask him first?"

I had a bad feeling about this, already having a good idea what Linda was thanking me for.

Mark didn't look the least bit regretful when he sat to my side, saying, "One of the guys who was participating tonight is ill so pulled out. I said you wouldn't mind filling in. You know how important this evening is to Mum."

"Oh, Mark," Linda said, exasperated. "I swear you were dropped on your head as a baby. I'm so sorry, Trey. If you can't do it, I'll understand. But I'll make sure Mark bids extra high for you."

The whole time she spoke, my eyes remained on Mark, that grin still on his face. He was a shit at times, and he knew full well I wouldn't let Linda down. "Throw in weekly back massages and breakfast in bed and it's a deal."

Laughter from his parents and sister surrounded us, and I cocked my brow at Mark.

"Deal," he said immediately. His gaze softened a little then and he leaned into my space. "I'm a dick, I know, but I promise to make it up to you."

"Too right you will."

He reached out and squeezed my leg and clasped my hand, pulling it to his lips and dotting a kiss there. Of course, my heart flipped over itself. The guy knew how to play me something fierce.

"Wonderful." Linda clapped her hands once and I glanced over at her. "You're up second, and I've made sure Mark's not on till eight, so you have plenty of time to return to your seats and bid."

Second? My chest restricted a little at that. I'd have to be standing up in front of all of these people. I shuddered inwardly, despite knowing that when it came to Mark being on stage, I planned to make somewhat of a spectacle of myself by getting down on one knee.

I inhaled deeply, strengthening my resolve as I stood and followed Linda to the back of the staging area, trying not to worry about stumbling or making a fool of myself.

When Linda left me with an arm squeeze and a "Good luck," I watched from the side of the stage as the emcee got the evening started. A young guy, a good few years younger than me, was already on stage and receiving some impressive bids. While nerves came alive in my stomach, not eager for the spotlight, I smiled.

Last year, Linda's foundation had raised a lot, and over one of countless family dinners, she'd talked to me in depth about the funds and how they were distributed. With that in mind, it was kinda nice to be involved, especially as I planned for this to be the final year Mark and I be involved other than buying a ticket.

"Okay, you're next," a young woman next to me said, taking me by surprise. As if seeing my hesitation, she smiled. "You'll be great."

I nodded and stepped out on to the stage once I was introduced. The lights were blinding, making it difficult to see the room and the audience. Focusing on walking and not tripping over, I kept my smile in place and stopped in the middle where an X was stuck to the floor.

Not really paying attention to the emcee, I glanced out, smiling and hoping I didn't look deranged with how fixed it was. I wanted to squint to see past the lights, but I didn't think that would help. The good news was that bidding was going on, but with paddles being used, I had no idea who was bidding.

"Twenty-eight thousand" was called through the crowd and I grinned, recognising Linda's voice immediately. A round of applause followed that, and when the claps wore off, a new weird sort of energy filled the room. The emcee didn't speak and I glanced in the guy's direction. My eyes sprung open wide, my heart pounded, stumbling to find a rhythm to settle on, and the whole time, my gaze remained on the man stepping towards me on the stage.

I gasped for breath, inhaling much-needed air, dragging it in and trying to get my brain to kick-start. Mark's gaze was intense, and 100 percent focussed on me. I couldn't look away, captured in his hold on me.

By the time he was a few short metres before me, I took in his small smile, then my gaze landed on his paddle which he held before him.

Marry Me?

The butterflies were gone, in their place a tsunami of emotion built, vying for space. It spread throughout my body, reaching my heart, filling it to the point I thought it would burst free. The only escape it had was in my ragged breaths and the tears springing into my eyes.

Within touching distance, Mark dropped to one knee, his eye contact never straying from mine. "You're it for me, Trey. Always and forever. I'll always bid on you, bid on us and our life together. Be mine and marry me?" I spotted an open box in his hand and he reached up and gripped my palm.

My nods came thick and fast before he'd finished speaking. He squeezed my hand and made to stand, but I stopped him. "Wait."

Mark's eyes widened at my request, the first time a little hesitation appeared in the depth of his eyes. I ignored the slight murmurs around us, the clapping that had died out with my request, and when I dropped to one knee, eye level with Mark, I finally smiled at his wide-eyed expression.

I released his hand a moment and tugged the ring box out of my pocket, opening it. Mark's eyes followed the movement, the surprise on his face perfect. Immediately, his eyes connected with my own. "For real?"

I nodded, laughing lightly. Tears swam in my eyes, but this development helped to keep them at bay.

A few gasps erupted from the crowd, and I was pretty sure I heard Linda crying. My focus remained true on the man before me. "I love you. There's no one else I want or need but you. You'll always find a way to catch me when I stumble, and I promise to absolutely do the same for you. You have my heart. Always. And yes," I finally answered, "I'll marry you, but I really wanted to ask, marry me?"

Mark's laughter drifted between us, happy and light. Emotion entered his eyes and he nodded. "Absolutely yes." His lips were on mine before I could take a breath, the kiss gentle, soft, and filled with the millions of unspoken words still to share.

I pulled away first, eager to get my ring on his finger. Half-lidded eyes stared back at me and he grinned when I took his hand and helped him with his ring. Immediately, my own ring sat on my finger, feeling both different and wonderful.

By the time we stood, applause rang around the room, along with cheers, and I glanced out, eyes adjusting to see Mark's family racing over to us.

Happiness swept through me. "You think we can leave the stage now?" I whispered.

Mark nodded. "Definitely, and we'll never need to be on here again." He pressed a kiss against the ring on my hand, sent a quick wave to the audience who were finally settling themselves down after us taking over the event, and we headed to his waiting family off to the side.

Wrapped in love and acceptance from his family and then later his friends, I sighed, contentment chasing my breath. Life with Mark was beyond anything I'd ever dreamed of, and without a doubt I knew he felt the same way about me. I pressed a kiss to his cheek when we sat back at the table, earning me a look of absolute love.

This moment right here was what everyone deserved. And I was grateful as hell that all those months ago, a stumble on a plane ensured that this man's lips would be the last I'd ever kiss.

The Outback Boys series continues with Aiden's story in *Bounce (#2)*.

Want more M/M Aussie romances? Check out *Thicker Than Water* for a smouldering, action-packed urban fantasy romance. Looking for another contemporary read? Then *Not Used To Cute* is the perfect Aussie book to also check out. Plus, don't forget *Realigned* is always free—my sexy cowboy romance.

ACKNOWLEDGMENTS

A huge thanks to the Winter Wonderland group, and Lucy Lennox especially, whose brainchild the event this book first featured was. Book 2, *Bounce*, was already partially written before this group was created, giving me a much-needed push to not only finish a story that's been on the back burner for over a year, but it nudged me into writing *Stumble*.

As always, I adore my Hot Tree family, and Claire from BookSmith, who provide me with daily support. You're the best!

ABOUT THE AUTHOR

I live and breathe all things book related. Usually with at least three books being read and two WiPs being written at the same time, life is merrily hectic. I tend to do nothing by halves, so I happily seek the craziness and busyness life offers.

Living on my small property in Queensland with my human family as well as my animal family of cows, chooks, and dogs, I really do appreciate the beauty of the world around me and am a believer that love truly is love.

To check for updates head to my website:
https://beccaseymour.com
You can sign up for my newsletter here:
https://landing.mailerlite.com/webforms/
landing/r9f0i4
Plus, join my Facebook group, which I share with the awesome Louisa Masters here:
https://www.facebook.com/
groups/rommancewithbeccalouisa

facebook.com / beccaseymourauthor
twitter.com / beccaseymour_
instagram.com / authorbeccaseymour
bookbub.com / authors / becca-seymour